"Honey, are you ready for bed?" Maizie channeled her inner seductress as she struck a pose in the door.

No response.

"Clayton. Did you hear me?"

"Sure," he answered, but didn't take his eyes off the T.V. screen. "Let me catch the rest of the news and I'll be right with you."

The moron would rather watch the weather than make love? If that didn't beat all! She counted to ten and decided to give him one more chance.

All Southern belles had an arsenal of tricks, and Maizie was no exception. She treated her oblivious husband to a little swish, a more pronounced sashay and a coup de grâce—a naughty hip grind—all done right in front of him for maximum effect.

Nothing. Absolutely nothing. This was war. Clay didn't know it yet, but he was going to live to rue this day.

Dear Reader,

Have you ever thought about spicing up your love life? After more than twenty years of marriage, Mary Stuart "Maizie" Walker is ready for a little rockin' and rollin',' and that's when she comes up with the perfect plan. She's going to make her hubby jealous by flirting with the handsome tennis pro. However, that scheme, like the best-laid plans of mice and Southern belles, backfires—big-time.

Welcome back to Magnolia Bluffs, the hometown of Maizie and her cohorts in mischief—Liza and Kenni. There's never a dull moment when the Steel Magnolias are up to their antics, and this time Mama and the aunts get involved. *The Man She Married* is fun, it's funky and I hope it makes you laugh out loud.

Ann

Here's a great snack for football parties.

Georgia Munchies

6 cups popped popcorn
1 (6-ounce) bag corn chips
2 cups bite-size pretzels
1 (3-ounce) can Chinese noodles
1 stick margarine
2 teaspoons Worcestershire
1 teaspoon Tabasco
1/8 teaspoon garlic powder

Combine popcorn, chips, pretzels and noodles. Melt margarine; stir in sauces and garlic. Pour over popcorn mix and toss to coat. Bake at 250 degrees for 1 hour. Stir every 15 minutes. Cool and store in airtight containers. Yields 12 cups.

The Man She Married

ANN DeFEE

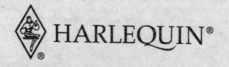

TORONTO • NEW YORK • LONDON
AMSTERDAM • PARIS • SYDNEY • HAMBURG
STOCKHOLM • ATHENS • TOKYO • MILAN • MADRID
PRAGUE • WARSAW • BUDAPEST • AUCKLAND

Recycling programs
for this product may
not exist in your area.

ISBN-13: 978-0-373-75252-2
ISBN-10:   0-373-75252-0

THE MAN SHE MARRIED

Copyright © 2009 by Ann DeFee.

All rights reserved. Except for use in any review, the reproduction or
utilization of this work in whole or in part in any form by any electronic,
mechanical or other means, now known or hereafter invented, including
xerography, photocopying and recording, or in any information storage
or retrieval system, is forbidden without the written permission of the
publisher, Harlequin Enterprises Limited, 225 Duncan Mill Road,
Don Mills, Ontario M3B 3K9, Canada.

This is a work of fiction. Names, characters, places and incidents are
either the product of the author's imagination or are used fictitiously,
and any resemblance to actual persons, living or dead, business
establishments, events or locales is entirely coincidental.

This edition published by arrangement with Harlequin Books S.A.

® and TM are trademarks of the publisher. Trademarks indicated with
® are registered in the United States Patent and Trademark Office, the
Canadian Trade Marks Office and in other countries.

www.eHarlequin.com

Printed in U.S.A.

ABOUT THE AUTHOR

Ann DeFee's debut novel, *A Texas State of Mind* (Harlequin American Romance), was a double finalist in the 2006 Romance Writers of America's prestigious RITA® Awards.

Drawing on her background as a fifth-generation Texan, Ann loves to take her readers into the sassy and sometimes wacky world of a small Southern community. As an air force wife with twenty-three moves under her belt, she's now settled in her tree house in the Pacific Northwest with her husband, their golden retriever and two very spoiled cats. When she's not writing, you can probably find her on the tennis court or in the park with her walking group.

Ann loves to hear from her readers, so please visit her Web site at www.ann-defee.com. Or contact her by snail mail at P.O. Box 97313, Tacoma, WA 98497.

Books by Ann DeFee

HARLEQUIN AMERICAN ROMANCE
1076—A TEXAS STATE OF MIND
1115—TEXAS BORN
1155—SOMEWHERE DOWN IN TEXAS
1176—GEORGIA ON HIS MIND
1185—THE PERFECT TREE
     "One Magic Christmas"
1202—GOIN' DOWN TO GEORGIA

HARLEQUIN EVERLASTING LOVE
16—SUMMER AFTER SUMMER

Don't miss any of our special offers. Write to us at the following address for information on our newest releases.

Harlequin Reader Service
U.S.: 3010 Walden Ave., P.O. Box 1325, Buffalo, NY 14269
Canadian: P.O. Box 609, Fort Erie, Ont. L2A 5X3

This book is dedicated to the terrific folks at Harlequin who make our books a reality, with special kudos to Megan Long, Paula Eykelhof and Kathleen Scheibling. And a special thanks to my good friends Geri Krotow and Debbie Macomber.

Without the help and support of these extraordinary ladies I'd probably still be writing comprehensive plans. And this is a whole lot more fun!

Chapter One

"Do these jeans make my butt look fat?" Mary Stuart "Maizie" Walker *realized* she was asking a no-win question. And she knew she was being unfair—honestly she did—but the devil on her shoulder kept poking her.

Clay, her husband of twenty-two years, glanced up from the paper. The expression on his was face was classic "deer in the headlights." It was so typical it was almost humorous, and that partially explained why Maizie was going out of her way to shake up their "we've been married forever" life. She was determined to inject some rockin' and rollin' into their intimacy.

Intellectually she recognized she was in the middle of an empty-nest crisis. Hannah, her baby, was a freshman at Emory University in Atlanta. And although the school was only fifty miles from Magnolia Bluffs, she was missing her daughter like crazy. Okay, she wasn't being rational, but who could blame her?

"Uh, well, uh." Clay threw up his hands. "What do you want me to say? Lately, I can't seem to get it right. I feel like I've walked into the middle of a pop quiz and I didn't even know I was *in* school."

Poor Clay. Maizie had loved him her entire adult life, and a good portion of her adolescence. That love hadn't changed, so why was she being such a shrew? Lord love a duck, was she going into early menopause? Or was she merely losing her mind? For months there had been this pervasive sense of dissatisfaction that she couldn't seem to shake.

Stop it right this minute! She had a wonderful life and it was time to get a grip.

"No answer?" Clay asked before giving her the same sexy wink she'd fallen for in the sixth grade.

"No," Maizie admitted. She sat on his lap and put her arms around his neck. "I'm sorry. I'm just feeling funky."

Clay nestled her against his chest. "I know, baby. I know."

And he probably did. Over the years they'd achieved a Spocklike mind meld. Besides completing each other's sentences, they were also able to communicate without saying a word.

Clay nuzzled her neck, paying special attention to her favorite erogenous zone behind her ear. When he did that Maizie couldn't help but melt into a puddle of lust.

He was a laid-back kind of guy with a quirky sense of humor, which was only one of the many things she loved about him. Clay had the same twinkly blue eyes and shaggy blond hair that had caught Maizie's attention in elementary school. Way back when he thought a spit wad attack was foreplay. Thank goodness his technique had improved since then.

"I don't have to be at the shop until ten." Maizie tried

her best flirtatious smile. "Do you think you could stick around for a while?"

Clay gave her neck one last nibble. "Oh, honey, I wish I could. Honest to God I do. But I have an important meeting with the Department of Transportation people." Clay and his partner, Harvey, owned Magnolia Bluff's premier engineering firm. "I can't miss it." He kissed the end of her nose. "I'll make it up to you, I promise."

"No big deal," Maizie said as she jumped up and sashayed out of the room.

CLAY WATCHED MAIZIE walk away. Despite what she said, he knew it *was* a big deal. He was a smart guy and he'd been married long enough to recognize high dudgeon when he saw it. Lately he seemed to be screwing up all the time. Everything he tried blew up in his face, especially when it came to his wife, the sexiest, funniest, most appealing woman he'd ever met.

Maizie reminded him of a 1950s movie star—a cross between Marilyn Monroe and Pamela Anderson, sans surgical enhancements. She griped about the few pounds she'd gained, but as far as Clay was concerned her curves were perfect.

Straying had never entered his mind. His theory was why go out for chicken nuggets when you had cordon bleu at home, but lately, whew! The trouble had started when Hannah left for college and the situation was rapidly going downhill.

Maizie was the owner/operator of Miss Scarlett's Boudoir. Her boutique was the emporium of all things girly in Magnolia Bluffs, Georgia, and it truly was the happening place. So if boredom wasn't the problem, what was it—other than missing her baby?

Then Clay froze as a horrible thought struck him. Was his wife getting tired of *him?* Maizie and Hannah were his entire world. He didn't think he could survive without them.

God, he didn't need this right now, not on top of the trouble at work. Thinking about the debacle at the office made him want to beat his head against the wall.

Then Clay had a brilliant idea. Even he could admit it was time to call in an expert and who better than her fraternal twin, Liza. They were about as simpatico as two people could be.

Add in their cousin Kenni Whittaker and you had the Three Musketeers. Yep, Liza and Kenni would know what to do.

Pleased that he had a game plan, Clay grabbed his car keys and headed off to work. He'd call Liza when he had a spare minute—not that he had many of those.

Chapter Two

It had been a lousy morning. Maizie hated fighting with Clay, but sometimes it felt like a black mood hijacked her brain. And when that happened, dealing with it was worse than getting rid of a bad case of fleas.

Maizie was doing some deep breathing exercises in the back room of the Boudoir, getting ready to put on her happy face, when she heard a screech followed by a crash. Then someone growled, "Let's go outside and settle this." That was something you'd hear at the Honky-Tonk Inn, not at Miss Scarlett's.

Enough was enough. Damn it all! Maizie threw her half-eaten Godiva bar in the cabinet and stomped out into the shop. A quick look revealed there wasn't much to worry about. The combatants were two middle-aged women armed with nothing more lethal than their razor-sharp tongues. Her employees, PJ and Bambi, stood by helplessly.

"What in the Sam Hill do you two think you're doing?" Maizie demanded, slamming her hands on her hips for emphasis. She had at least a seven-inch height advantage on both women and she wasn't afraid to use it. "This isn't a junior high cafeteria."

Sue Belle Pennington and Lucy Albright had been mortal enemies since cheerleading tryouts in the eighth grade. Add the unfortunate fact that neither had the sense God gave a turnip—and voilà—they were an incident waiting to happen.

Maizie tapped her toe. If they weren't going to behave they could get out of *her* store. "I'm waiting for an explanation, and it had better be good."

"She, she…" Sue Belle pointed a bony finger at her archenemy. "She thinks she's smart enough to run the Girl Scout cookie sale. God knows she came out of the shallow end of the gene pool." The commentary was bad enough, but her wicked-witch cackle was the icing on the cake.

Lucy lunged for Sue Belle, ready to draw blood, but Maizie grabbed her in midflight.

"You're having a catfight, in *my* store, over who's going to be the *cookie mama?*" Maizie would've slammed their heads together if she'd thought it would do any good.

Sue Belle raised her hand in preparation for a rude gesture, but obviously reconsidered when Maizie shot her a lethal glare.

Lucy, however, didn't know when to quit. "Her mama stole the Brownie money when we were in third grade. And everyone knows the apple doesn't fall far from the tree." She accompanied her snarky remark with a smirk.

Oops! The ass whoopin' was about to commence.

"Grab Sue Belle," Maizie yelled to PJ, praying that

her assistant manager would be able to restrain the enraged woman. Considering Sue Belle outweighed PJ by at least seventy-five pounds there wasn't much hope of that.

"Call my brother-in-law." Maizie tossed the cordless phone to Bambi, her after-school clerk. "Tell him to send someone over immediately."

Zack Maynard, Liza's husband, was the county sheriff. Sometimes it was handy to have a relative with a badge.

"Stop it right this minute!" Maizie screamed. Lordy, she hadn't yelled that loud since her own cheerleading days. But it worked. Everyone in the shop went stock-still.

"Sit down. I will not tolerate a brawl in my store."

Lucy sputtered and Sue Belle straightened her blouse where PJ had latched on to her arm. Although the combatants looked as if they'd rather have tea with Satan, they reluctantly complied, settling on opposite ends of the brocade Victorian fainting couch near the change rooms. The cease-fire, however, didn't stop them from shooting baleful looks at each other.

"The dispatcher said someone would be here soon. But not to worry, the doughnut shop's not too far away." Bambi punctuated her report with a typical teenage giggle.

From her lips to God's ears.

Ten minutes later Deputy Bubba Watson strolled in, a trail of white powder dribbled down his uniform, and it wasn't cocaine. The poor man wasn't the sharpest crayon in the box, but he was the law. And if he could scare the bejeezus out of the nitwits, everything would be fine.

"What's this I hear about a fight?" he drawled, snapping his suspenders in unison with the popping of his gum.

Maizie indicated the two women. "There they are."

"Whatcha gals up to?" Bubba asked. His interrogation techniques weren't exactly FBI approved.

Sue Belle started to speak, but Lucy interrupted. "She wants to—"

Not to be outdone, Sue Belle launched into her own spiel.

"That's it! Bubba, get them out of here before I do something I'll regret," Maizie demanded. She turned to Lucy and Sue Belle. "You two are permanently banned from the Boudoir. Do not darken this door again. Do you hear me? Never ever come in here again."

"Aw, Maizie. Don't be that way," Sue Belle wailed.

She was on the verge of tears, but that was too darned bad.

"Yeah." Lucy never had been able to keep her mouth shut. "If we can't shop at the Boudoir, we'll have to drive to Atlanta to find decent stuff. You can't really mean it."

"Oh, I do. Believe me."

Lucy's next words sealed her fate. "I'll sue you. Sure as shootin' I will."

Maizie managed to suppress a belly laugh. "Go ahead. My lawyer's a lot meaner than yours."

Cousin Kenni's husband, Win, was a former member of the D.C. legal scene. He was also Magnolia Bluff's newest and finest attorney and even though he specialized in criminal actions, he was perfectly capable of handling himself in civil court. That man could jump into a pool of sharks and come out without a scratch.

"Bring it on, baby." Maizie waved her fingers in the universal sign for "come and get it."

Bubba might've been a little slow, but even he recognized a good exit line. "Okay, ladies, let's go." He indicated the door. "One at a time, please." He gave Maizie a conspiratorial wink and a piece of advice before he escorted the offenders out. "Be good, now, ya hear?"

Maizie plopped on the couch, suddenly aware that her knees were knocking. "I can't wait to tell Clay. He won't believe this."

"Such dimwits." PJ shook her head in disgust. "Can't you just picture them rolling around on the floor and yankin' each other's hair out?"

PJ had been working for Maizie since she graduated from high school. When she wasn't helping run the boutique she was the happily married mother of two little mop-heads. A chubby version of Rachael Ray with curly blond hair and Hershey-brown eyes, PJ was as cute as a speckled pup. Plus, she had a ready smile, a sharp wit and the common sense of Solomon.

"On that note I think we deserve some chocolate." Maizie strolled to the back room and returned with a box of Belgian candy.

"Eat up," she said. "To heck with the calories." Maizie saved her "good stuff" for emergencies and celebrations, and this situation definitely qualified.

THE REMAINDER OF THE afternoon went by without incident. It was a typical Friday at the Boudoir—purchases were made, returns were processed and customers were accommodated.

The gold-leafed sign on the window read Miss Scarlett's Boudoir, and if the inventory was any indication, Miss Scarlett had had herself a grand old time. It was a treasure trove of lace pillows, frothy undergarments and feminine apparel. Even the bell above the door sounded girly.

It was kitschy, it was fun and it had something for everyone. The blue-hairs loved the bath and beauty selection and the teens were hot for the trendy collection of jeans. Best of all, Maizie and PJ were known throughout the area for the exclusive line of French cosmetics they applied with a flourish. If you were in the market for a makeover, the Boudoir was definitely the place to go.

Under normal circumstances the boutique was a fantastic place to work, but this day had been a doozey and Maizie was dead on her feet.

"PJ, would you close the shop today?" she asked. "I need to run by the grocery store. We're having a family football party at my house tomorrow."

"No problem. It's almost six o'clock anyway."

"I won't be in tomorrow. Bambi and Jerry Sue will be here to help you."

"Gotcha. Don't worry about a thing."

MAIZIE PULLED INTO THE Piggly Wiggly parking lot. She was hoping to run in and out quickly but the chances of that happening in Magnolia Bluffs—where everyone knew everyone else's business and loved to discuss it—were slim.

Before Maizie could make it to the cash register, Laverne Hightower, the town's rumor maven, had managed to share a play-by-play of her gallbladder attack. Not to be outdone, Shirley Smith had launched into a full rundown on her daughter's wedding preparations. And *everyone* wanted to talk about the commotion at the Boudoir. The next time Maizie needed food she'd go to the big box store out on the bypass.

By the time the groceries were bought, the errands were run and the day was over, she was ready to pull her hair out. No doubt about it—today had been one of *those* days.

Maizie breathed a sigh of relief as she pulled up to the detached garage behind her rambling white turn-of-the-century bungalow. Her home was typically Southern with green shutters, a wraparound veranda and a trellis of honeysuckle.

When things got too hectic, Maizie loved to sit on the porch swing with a frosty glass of sweet tea and watch the world go by. It was her way of sweeping out the mental cobwebs. However that was an indulgence for another day.

"Clay!" Maizie called as she dropped her purse and a bag of canned goods on the kitchen table. "I need some help."

The television was blaring in the family room, and hubby dear was missing in action.

"Clay, where are you?" Maizie was perfectly capable of carrying in the rest of the food, but it was the principle of the thing.

"Clayton!"

That apparently got his attention. "What do you need, Babes?" he answered, not bothering to move away from the television.

"I want some help with the groceries."

"Can you wait a minute? I'm watching something."

Maizie stomped into the family room to see what was so important. *Bass fishing?* Clay wasn't waiting for a touchdown to be scored or a home run to be hit. No—he was sitting in his favorite leather chair with his feet propped on the ottoman, watching some guy in an expensive boat troll for *fish*.

Maizie was normally even-tempered—except when she was in a snit, and she didn't really count that—but she grabbed the remote, hit the Off button and marched out. Making a grand exit was a talent she'd learned at her mama's knee, and she happened to be darned good at it.

CRAP. CLAY KNEW HE was in a mess of trouble, again. What had he done this time? All he'd wanted to do was see if Skeeter Jackson would win the tournament and the hundred-thousand-dollar prize. He could have used that kind of cash himself. It would go a long way toward solving at least one of his problems.

But immersing himself in that pipe dream had only irritated his sweetie, so clearly Clay had to make amends. Should he go with the "I'm so sorry, I'm an insensitive jerk" defense? That usually worked, especially if he followed up with some heavy necking—and a promise to do the dishes, take out the trash, clean the bathroom, yada, yada, yada.

"I'm sorry." Clay was honestly remorseful. He hated upsetting Maizie.

"Why don't you sit down and let me get you a Coke," he suggested. Without waiting for an answer he retrieved a soft drink and handed it to her.

Clay was about to give himself a big pat on the back. Then he saw his wife's face. Something was drastically wrong, and it had nothing to do with bringing in the groceries.

"Clay." Maizie sat at the pine trestle table, rubbing the cold can against her face. "Is this all we have to look forward to?"

That question scared Clay silly. When your wife got philosophical, all hell was about to break loose.

Chapter Three

It was a beautiful October Saturday, the leaves had changed, the air was crisp, and the University of Georgia was in the hunt for a national football title. Everyone in town was infected by gridiron fever and the Walkers were usually no exception. Back in the dark ages, Maizie had been a UGA cheerleader and Clay had been a star linebacker on the team. Needless to say, they were huge fans.

Regardless of the hoopla, Maizie was having a hard time getting into the "rah rah" mood. In fact, she was in more of a "kick 'em in the knee" frame of mind. On that depressing thought she answered the annoying ring of the phone, hoping it was a telemarketer, not someone she'd actually have to talk to.

"What's wrong?" Only her twin would pick up on trouble from a simple hello.

"Nothing. I'm just feeling out of sorts." Maizie normally shared everything with her sister, but this situation felt different.

"Is Hannah okay?"

Maizie chuckled, thinking about her flower child.

"She's fine, but her dad almost flipped when she told him she was considering majoring in pottery."

Maizie was inclined to be a bit zany. Liza, on the other hand, was a lawyer and practical to the max, so she probably didn't understand the pottery thing, either.

"Well, uh." Liza paused. "I didn't know they offered that major at Emory."

"It was news to me, too," Maizie said. "That's why I decided to worry about it later. Next week she'll have changed her mind again."

A fan of *Gone With the Wind,* Maizie had long ago adopted Scarlett's fiddle-dee-dee attitude, and so far it had worked perfectly. "What time are you guys coming over?" She could segue at the drop of a hat.

"The game starts at six, so how does five or five-thirty sound?"

"That works. Kenni and Win won't be here until around seven. He has to meet with a client."

"The only thing they'll miss is the pregame hype. What do you want me to bring?" Liza asked.

A casual observer might assume Liza had forgotten about her sister's funk, but Maizie knew better.

"See you soon," Liza said. "Oh, by the way, don't get smug. We're going to have a little chat when I get there."

Darn, that girl was like a dog with a juicy bone. No wonder she was an attorney.

THE GUYS WERE BONDING over the pregame show and pigging out on chips and salsa. That allowed Liza carte blanche to start the inquisition. Before she pulled out the thumb screws, though, she grabbed two bottles of

Heineken from the fridge and a couple of frosty mugs from the freezer.

"Sit." Liza handed Maizie a beer as a peace offering. "Now spill your guts."

Maizie was a smart girl so she could tell when it was time to surrender. Liza might be no bigger than gnat's eyelash, but she could be real mean. Well, maybe determined would be a better description, but whatever— Liza almost always got her way.

Mama said their stubborn streak was the only thing the twins shared. Liza was petite and dark while Maizie looked more like a Viking goddess. They were so different it was sometimes hard to believe they'd actually shared a womb.

Maizie reluctantly sat down. "I honestly don't know what my problem is, I wish I did. At first I thought it was empty-nest syndrome, but lately I've been wondering if it's the twenty-two-year itch." She shrugged. "All I know is that I'm feelin' a bit blue." Maizie didn't mention her stale love life. Even for a twin that was too much information.

"Oh, honey. You need something to cheer you up. You're simply having a hormonal crisis." Liza raised a finger in her favorite "aha" signal. "I have an idea. We'll talk Kenni into going with us to Lennox Square for a girls' day out. We can rummage through Nordstrom's shoe section and then indulge in some decadent chocolate. Think about it, imported chocolate and sexy sandals. What more could you want?"

Maizie couldn't resist a grin. "Are we talking fattening and expensive?"

"Absolutely." Liza held up her hand for a high five.

Although Maizie wasn't sure a spending spree would do the trick, she was willing to try. Pessimism was new and rather unwelcome territory.

The party was a smashing success, partially because of the company, but equally because UGA won the Southeastern Conference championship. The next step was to wait for the football bowl selections to see if UGA would be fighting to be number one in the nation. For die-hard college football fans that was a huge deal.

The kitchen was clean, the family room had been tidied and the company had gone. Clay was on a football high and Maizie was feeling, well, to put it delicately, a bit amorous. Or to be blunt, she was ready to fool around.

A long bath, a flute of bubbly, a sexy teddy and a spray of perfume later, she was hot to trot. But was Clay?

"Honey, are you ready for bed?" Maizie channeled her inner seductress as she struck a pose in the door.

No response.

"Clayton. Did you hear me?"

When he didn't respond Maizie decided it was time for more action and less talk. She walked slowly over to the couch and seductively nibbled on the back of his neck.

"Let me catch the rest of the news and I'll be right with you," he said, not taking his eyes off the screen.

"What?" Maizie couldn't believe she'd been re-buffed. The moron would rather watch the weather than make love? If that didn't beat all! She counted to ten and decided to give him one more chance.

All Southern belles had an arsenal of tricks, and Maizie was no exception. She treated her oblivious husband to a little swish, a more pronounced sashay and the coup de grace, a naughty hip grind, all done right in front of him for maximum effect.

Nothing. Absolutely nothing! This was war. Clay didn't know it yet, but he would live to rue this day.

Maizie stalked to the bedroom and pulled on an oversize Atlanta Braves T-shirt and a pair of faded boxer shorts. To hell with sexy.

Then she had a brilliant idea. She'd make Clay pea-green jealous. Not that she'd ever do anything more than flirt, of course.

Clay was the only man for her, but a little flirtation couldn't hurt. All she had to do was show him that other men found her attractive. It was a surefire way to jump start the passion.

It sounded simple, but could she really pull it off? Magnolia Bluff's selection of single, desirable men was limited. Who was she kidding? It was almost nonexistent. Kenni and Liza had managed to find a couple of supersexy guys, but Zack and Win were imports. The pickin's were slim when it came to the home-grown product.

So, where could she find a guy, preferably someone under sixty who still had his teeth? This would take some thought, but she'd never shied away from a challenge.

Once that was decided, Maizie padded to the kitchen for a snack. Clay was still glued to the TV in the family room. What she really wanted to do was to curl up in his lap and run her fingers through his hair, but that wasn't on the agenda, not after the last rejection. They had to get some zing back in their life, and she knew just how to do it.

Pigging out on a glass of cold milk and a chocolate cookie seemed a good strategy to get some perspective. Unfortunately, the sugar rush gave way to a
smidgen of doubt.

Was this jealousy scheme a flash of brilliance or was
it one of the silliest ideas she'd ever dreamed up? Only
time would tell.

CLAY TRIED TO IGNORE his sense of impending disaster,
but the banging and muttering in the kitchen didn't
help. Once again, he'd made Maizie mad and that
honestly hadn't been his intention.

The party had been sheer hell. It had taken every
ounce of energy Clay had to smile and prattle on about
football and national championships. Especially since he
hadn't slept more than three hours a night for the past two
weeks.

Every time he closed his eyes all he could envision
was the bankruptcy court and what would happen to
their employees if they went under. He should come
clean with Maizie. They'd always shared everything,
but he and his partner had made such stupid, naive
mistakes, he was embarrassed to tell her.

It would all work out. It had to. God, he was exhausted. That was the last thought Clay had before he
fell asleep in his chair.

Chapter Four

When Monday finally rolled around Maizie couldn't wait for her workday to start. She needed some info and there was no better place to get it than her shop. The right guy for the jealousy gig was out there, all she had to do was find him.

Maizie fluffed her hair, put on her best Miss Georgia third runner-up smile and prepared to greet her customers. Jeannine Crabtree was scheduled for a makeover. The crazy old bat expected a miracle. Too bad miracles were in short supply.

The good news, if there was any, was that Jeannine was related to at least a quarter of the people in town. So if the perfect guy was around, she'd know about him. The only question was whether she'd share.

"Maizie? Are you here?" PJ called as she opened the front door. Hmm, that girl could charm anyone—even Jeannine Crabtree. She could interrogate the old witch without her even realizing what was happening.

"I'm here." Maizie threw a smock over her dress. "I'll be out in just a sec."

"I stopped in at the bakery on my way to work. I

brought beignets." PJ displayed a white sack that had a slight smudge of grease on the bottom. "They're hot."

Maizie groaned. "You're a wicked, wicked woman. You know I'm trying to lose a couple of pounds."

"Fiddlesticks, you look fantastic. I wish I had a little more, um…" PJ made a bouncy motion with her hands in front of her chest. "Cleavage," she finished with a giggle.

Maizie grabbed the bag, retrieved one of the New Orleans doughnuts and took a big bite. "Oh my God, this is better than sex." She almost purred in ecstasy. "I think I'll give you a raise."

PJ arched one eyebrow. "Really?"

"No, not really. But if you do Jeannine Crabtree's makeover I'll be eternally grateful."

Village legend had it that you could walk into Miss Scarlett's Boudoir looking like Cinderella's ugly stepsister and walk out as Carmen Electra. Maizie claimed it was all in the magic of a mascara wand. Whatever it was, women of all ages had turned into believers—even the crabby Ms. Crabtree.

PJ snorted. "I'll just bet you would. That woman's as mean as a junkyard dog. If I can stay out of her way, I do." She graced Maizie with her best insincere smile. "Sorry, my schedule is completely booked."

She didn't look a bit contrite. "Oh, all right." Maizie was a smart girl. She knew when to hold 'em and when to fold 'em.

"I almost forgot," PJ said as she prepared the cash register for the day. "I saw Liza at the post office this morning. She wants to meet you for lunch. You're supposed to call her at work."

"Thanks." Maizie picked up the cordless phone and punched in her twin's number.

"Liza Hender…Maynard speaking."

"Forget your name?"

"Up yours."

"That's not very lawyerly. You should try to be more professional." Maizie broke into giggles. She was the elder by a mere ten minutes but had embraced the role of big sister.

"Seriously, PJ said you want to do lunch. Where and when?"

"Hold on a second." Liza must have put her hand over the receiver because the voices were in the backyard muffled. Several seconds later she came back on the line. "Okay, that's taken care of. Don't you hate Monday morning crises?"

"Yep," Maizie said as she rummaged through her makeup kit. Multitasking was her specialty and spiffing up old lady Crabtree was going to require every trick she knew.

"Zack said there's a new barbecue place out near the highway. Do you want to try it?"

Maizie laughed. Today was the first day of her new diet and she'd already gorged herself on a deep-fried doughnut and now she was booked for some down-home barbecue. She could almost feel the fat cells multiplying on her derriere.

"Sure, why not? How about one o'clock? The noon rush should be over by then."

"I'll see you there," Liza said, and then almost as an afterthought she continued. "You might want to change into something old. I hear the food's pretty greasy."

Wonderful—big globs of grease, too. Just what she needed. On that cheerful note, the bell over the door heralded Ms. Crabtree's entrance.

"Okay. I've gotta go. See you soon." It was time to paste on a smile, pull out the white-glove manners and get on with life.

"Jeannine, how are you doin'? I haven't seen you in a month of Sundays." Maizie snapped a plastic cape open with a flourish. "Let's get you seated." She led her customer to a chair at the back of the boutique. "And make you beautiful."

Maizie could've sworn she'd heard PJ giggle, but when she looked over, her friend wore a benign smile.

Jeannine's face, on the other hand, was set in a perpetual scowl. Maybe there was something to the old wives' tale about frowning.

"Tell you what, Ms. Crabtree." Maizie smoothed some of the tension out of the older woman's forehead. "I'm going to give you a complimentary refresher mask. It'll make your skin as soft as a baby's bottom." And if she believed that, fish were going to start walking on their hind legs. Maizie slathered pink gel over her client's face, knowing it wouldn't do any good. In this case, she had to trust the placebo effect to get the job done.

"You relax while the mask dries. Don't talk or it'll crack." Maizie patted Jeannine's shoulder before strolling up front.

The only other customer was a woman with a baby in a pram. Maizie recognized her from the country club as one of Magnolia Bluff's newest transplants from Atlanta. She was petite, tan, blond, beautiful and stylishly dressed. Yep, this young matron had the potential to become a good customer—very good, indeed.

"Hi, I don't think we've met." One of the reasons Miss Scarlett's was so successful was the friendly atmosphere and personal service. "I'm Maizie Walker. I own the Boudoir."

The blonde extended her hand. "I'm so glad to meet you. I'm Paige Butler. I just love your store," she gushed. "And this town is terrific. We've only been here six months, but I feel as if I've known people forever."

Maizie glanced at PJ who was already loaded down with clothes that Paige had pulled off the racks in the few short minutes she'd been there. "If there's anything we can do, just let us know."

About that time the baby decided to join the party by letting out a wail.

"This is Ali," Paige introduced her daughter. She was obviously a proud parent. "She wants me to hold her all the time. My mama says I'm spoiling her but I can't help myself. I want to eat her up with a spoon."

Paige's daughter was a little dumpling. She was dressed all in pink and had a bow tied in her straw-colored hair.

"Do you mind if I pick her up?" Maizie tickled the baby's chin.

"Be my guest, please." Paige leaned over to readjust Ali's frilly dress. "I've been fantasizing about having fifteen minutes to myself."

"Ms. Crabtree's mask won't be ready for another ten minutes," Maizie told Paige, ignoring her client's grumbling in the background. "You two go on back to the dressing room and take your time."

"Yes, ma'am. I surely will. Thanks."

"Hey, Snookums," Maizie cooed to the baby. "What a little cutie you are." Ali's crying stopped almost immediately when Maizie lifted her out of the pram.

When Hannah was a baby Maizie had spent countless hours in an antique rocking chair she'd inherited from her Grammy Nelson. On a whim she'd put that lovely old chair in Miss Scarlett's. It was a beautiful addition to the décor as well as a perfect place for meditation when time allowed.

Maizie hummed and rocked while "Crabass's" mask hardened. Baby Ali fell asleep almost immediately. Maizie kissed the top of the baby's head, breathing in that sweet infant smell. There was nothing quite as innocent as a sleeping angel—awake was a different story. Ten peaceful minutes passed before Maizie admitted she had to do something about her client.

"PJ, Paige," she whispered, trying to be as quiet. "I need to take care of Ms. Crabtree."

"About time," Jeannine muttered.

"We're finished." PJ appeared with an armload of clothing. "Paige found lots of stuff," she said with a conspiratorial wink.

The young mom tucked the sleeping baby back into the pram and then pulled out her platinum American Express card. "Miz Walker, I can't tell you how much I appreciate you taking care of Ali."

"You're very welcome. We like to think of ourselves as a full-service operation. Now, if you'll excuse me I need to rinse off my client's mask."

"It's about time!" Mrs. C exclaimed when Maizie rejoined her.

Who could mistake those dulcet tones?

"Your skin's going to feel so soft that you won't mind the wait."

"I doubt that, but get on with it." The woman's gravelly voice was like fingernails on a chalkboard.

"Here we go." Maizie dabbed cleanser on Jeannine's face. Although she'd used her very best product, she couldn't see a dime's worth of difference.

"How is that? Doesn't your skin feel better?" Maizie turned Ms. Crabtree's chair toward the mirror.

She employed her best shopkeeper's voice to make certain she didn't utter anything particularly vile. Fortunately Maizie was saved by the bell—the one on the front door.

"Hey, Paige. How's it going?" The sound of a man's voice in Miss Scarlett's was unusual enough to be remarkable.

"Trip, my goodness, what are you doing here?" Paige sounded more like a lovesick teen than a mom. Or maybe a femme fatale.

When Maizie glanced up to check out what all the fuss was about, she was almost bowled over. Heavens to Betsy. The man talking to Paige could be Pierce Brosnan's younger brother. Even the vestal virgins would be cheering.

"Maizie, PJ, this is Trip Fitzgerald. He's the tennis coach at the country club. A bunch of us take lessons from him."

How interesting. No wonder the gorgeous hunk had tanned legs and broad shoulders. Trip Fitzgerald was exactly what the jealousy Cupid had ordered.

"Mr. Fitzgerald, you're new in town, too, right?" Maizie walked over to shake the newcomer's hand.

"Yes, ma'am. I've been here a month. I'm originally from Atlanta."

"Really. Well, welcome to Magnolia Bluffs. I hope we've been hospitable."

"I couldn't have asked for better." His grin was boyish, charming and damned near perfect—an orthodontist's dream.

"I need to get a birthday present for my mother," he said, looking around. "Several of my students said you're the best place in town."

"We certainly try to be. PJ—"

PJ almost tripped over her own feet racing to his side. "I can help you. What does your mom like? We have all kinds of pretties."

Before he could answer PJ was setting up a display of gift items that would be daunting for a seasoned shopper.

"Wow. That's quite a selection," he said, showcasing that grin again. "You ladies should come for tennis lessons. We have something for everyone. Groups, privates, semiprivates, you name it, we've got it. I think you'd really like it. It's good exercise and a great way to get a tan."

Maizie's mind was whirling a mile a minute—which generally landed her in a heap of trouble.

"Tennis lessons sound like exactly what I need." Were they ever.

Chapter Five

By noon Maizie was more than ready to tuck into a plate of juicy barbecue. It had been an interesting morning and she was tempted to treat herself to a frosty brew when she arrived early to meet Liza, but the thought of the carbs held her back.

The Crabtree ordeal and meeting Trip Fitzgerald had been followed by an "I've worn this at least a dozen times but now that it has a stain on the front I want to return it" and an "oh my, you mean you can't dry it on hot" complaint. Retail wasn't for sissies.

"Hey." Liza breezed in and gave her twin a hug. Lately she did everything with a spring in her step, and why not? She was a newlywed and madly in love. Not that Maizie was jealous or anything.

"Have you ordered?" she asked as she took a seat on the picnic table bench.

"Nope. I was waiting for you. I've been studying the menu and I think I'll go for the rib plate. See?" Maizie made a point of displaying her casual attire. "I changed into a T-shirt and jeans."

"Good girl. Let's see, what do I want?" Liza picked up the menu. "I think I'll try the rib plate, too. I—"

Before she could continue her thought, the waitress appeared armed with two huge containers of iced tea. "I was bettin' you gals would like a cold drink." She set the glasses down and pulled out her order pad. "The ribs are looking mighty good, and the peach cobbler—whew." She jokingly swiped her forehead. "I can put on five pounds just smellin' that stuff. It's downright sinful."

"Both of us want the rib platter. We'll discuss dessert later." Liza put the menu back behind the Tabasco sauce.

"Excellent choice. If you need anything else, give me a holler."

As soon as the waitress strolled off, Liza got down to why she'd wanted to do lunch.

"I've been putting a lot of thought into this, and I'm not convinced a shopping trip is what you need. I suspect there's something more serious going here. You're usually Little Miss Sunshine, and darn it, I want you to be happy again."

Maizie fiddled with the salt shaker. Should she or shouldn't she involve her twin? Not only was Liza a newlywed and desperately in love, she was also managing a huge property development project. She didn't have time to listen to Maizie moan about her marital status.

As a matter of fact, both Liza and Kenni were acting like love-struck loons. It was enough to make a person gag. Deep down, Maizie had to admit she was jealous. She and Clay used to share that kind of passion, and by gosh, she wanted it again.

"I've decided to take up tennis," she blurted.

"Tennis?" The look of confusion on Liza's face was

priceless. "You? Are you serious? The most strenuous thing you do is paint your nails."

"I'll have you know I played tennis in high school." Sure, she wasn't all that athletic, but Liza's comment ruffled her tail feathers.

"Oh, I forgot. You were a regular Martina Navratilova." Liza laughed at her own joke. "But what does that have to do with you being depressed?"

It was show time. Could she look her best friend, her twin in the face and lie? Or should she confide in her?

Confiding won, hands down. "Actually—" Maizie chewed on her bottom lip and screwed up her face.

Liza waited a few moments before speaking. "Actually what?"

"Actually, I have an ulterior motive."

"Duh." Liza crossed her arms. "Sweating isn't exactly your thing, and believe it or not, Sweet Cakes, when you exercise you glow, big time."

Every Southern girl knew that horses sweated, men perspired and women glowed. Maizie didn't bother to suppress her grimace. "I have some waterproof makeup. It stops up your pores so I don't normally wear it, but in this case I'll give it a shot."

"Look." Liza propped her chin on her hand. "What is this really all about?"

"I want to make Clay jealous."

"What?"

Maizie couldn't help feeling uncomfortable. "Clay's been ignoring me lately and I want him to realize that even though I'm middle-aged and plump, some men find me attractive."

Liza massaged her forehead. "Let me get this

straight. Please God, tell me I'm understanding this. You're planning to flirt with some dude on the tennis court to make Clay jealous?"

"Sort of."

Liza smacked her hand on the wooden table. "That's one of the dumbest schemes I've ever heard. Let me make one thing perfectly clear. You are a gorgeous woman. And plump, please! Women all over the country pay good money to have what God's given you."

"Don't get your knickers in a twist." Maizie leaned forward to let Liza in on a secret. "It's perfectly innocent. All I'm going to do is flirt with the new tennis pro. I checked him out, he's not married, or engaged or even dating anyone." She'd researched his relationship status by calling a friend who was a member of the club and a tennis fiend. "I'm certainly not planning to do anything other than get Clay's attention. How can anything go wrong?"

Chapter Six

Maizie had tried to sound confident when talking to Liza, but to be totally truthful she wasn't that sure her plan would work. And no matter what Liza said, she *had* gained several pounds—most of it right on her caboose.

However, she'd learned early in her beauty-pageant career that self-confidence could mask a ton of deficiencies, and fortunately that included a sizable derriere. It also required a certain amount of assistance, and in this case that meant a sexy, new tennis outfit.

Maizie and Clay were having breakfast when she volleyed the first shot in her "make my hubby jealous" campaign. "I'm going into Atlanta this morning to do some shopping."

"Okay," he answered.

"Just okay?" Why was she being so snarky? She frequently went to Atlanta, so why should this trip be different?

Clay put down the paper and shook his head.

"I'm sorry," Maizie said. "That was uncalled for."

He stared at her a few seconds and gently laid his

hand on her cheek. "I love you. You know that, don't you?"

The tenderness of his touch gave Maizie pause.

"Do you want me to come with you?"

"No! Uh, I mean, that's not necessary." Having him along would screw up the purpose of her shopping trip.

"Okay, if you're sure." Clay took her hand and kissed the tips of her fingers. Darn that man. He knew how to push every one of her buttons. She just wished he'd do it more often.

MAIZIE PULLED INTO THE parking lot of a tennis and golf superstore. It was a gigantic warehouse filled with sports equipment and clothing. She was more familiar with tony boutiques than places like the Tennis and Golfarama. Maizie was out of her element and didn't have a clue where to start.

"May I help you?" a clerk asked when she walked in. The young woman was tanned brunette wearing skintight warm-up gear. There wasn't an ounce of cellulite on that buff body.

"I need some tennis…uh…stuff."

"A racquet or clothes?"

"Both. Actually, I haven't played in years so I need everything, right down to the socks and bloomers."

Maizie's admission elicited a laugh from the saleswoman.

"I'm Cindi," she said, sticking her hand out for a shake.

Maizie would just bet she dotted the "i" with a heart.

"I'm sure we can find exactly what you need."

An hour later Maizie's credit card was limp from exhaustion and she was the proud owner of three new tennis outfits—all super sexy, of course—a top-of-the-line racquet and a pair of shoes guaranteed to put a spring in her step. Now all she needed was a plan, preferably one that had a chance of working.

MAIZIE'S FRIEND AT THE TENNIS club had also informed her that Trip Fitzgerald wasn't as young as he looked. He was actually closer to her age than to the young matrons who swarmed him like bees to honey.

But even so, Maizie had serious doubts about her ability to attract his attention. She wasn't twenty anymore, nor was she a size zero. Would he think of her as nothing more than a middle-aged groupie? The last thing she wanted was to come off as a pathetic cliché.

That would be incredibly humiliating.

Maizie was closing in on D-day, or T-day, as the case may be. She had the clothes, the racket, the shoes and she'd signed up for a series of lessons. The only thing she lacked was confidence. So naturally she made an impromptu visit to Cousin Kenni's salon, Permanently Yours.

Liza wasn't on board with her "make Clay jealous" plan. Perhaps Kenni would be more encouraging. What would Maizie do if her cousin jumped aboard the "ohmigod, that's a bad idea" bandwagon?

The Permanently Yours salon clientele ranged from senior citizens with tight perms to trendy adolescents and everyone in between. Like Miss Scarlett's Boudoir, it was a happening place.

"Hey, Toolie, what's up?" Maizie said as she walked in. Tallulah—aka Toolie—was an ex-pat from Atlanta, cute as a button and totally cool. Today she was sporting a spiked purple do that showed off her multiple earrings.

"Not much. Kenni's in the back doing Laverne Hightower's hair." She made a face to indicate her "ick" reaction.

"Gotcha." Maizie gave her a high five before heading toward the back of the salon.

"Hey, Raylene." Raylene was Kenni's other stylist. She specialized in the curly styles that were de rigueur with the over-eighty crowd. The hairdresser responded with a three-fingered wave.

"Hi, Kenni." Maizie smiled at her cousin in the mirror.

"Hello, Mrs. Hightower. How are you doing?" She knew when to suck up.

"Hello, Maizie Walker. How are you?"

"Fine, thank you, ma'am. You haven't been to the boutique lately. We're about to have a sale. You need to drop by, now 'ya hear? I always have gourmet coffee brewing."

"Gourmet, huh?" Laverne was renowned for grazing through the free samples at the Piggly Wiggly.

"Yes, ma'am."

Kenni secured the last pink foam roller and twirled her customer around. "I'm going to put you under the dryer now."

Kenni made sure Laverne was comfortable under a hood that looked like an old *Saturday Night Live* cone of silence and then crooked her finger at Maizie.

"Let's go to the office." The salon's office/break-room was really a storage area filled with boxes of beauty products, but there was a comfortable enough Goodwill couch and adequate refreshments.

"Sit, girl. You look like you're ready for a discussion."

"Yeah." Maizie moved a stack of hairstyle magazines and sat down in an old vinyl chair.

"How about something to drink?" Without waiting for an answer, Kenni rummaged in the refrigerator and came up with two cans of iced tea.

Before she could hand over the drink, Maizie blurted out, "Clay and I aren't exactly burning up the sheets anymore and I plan to do something about it."

Kenni froze. "Oo-kay." She put the cans back in the refrigerator and retrieved a pitcher of fluorescent green liquid.

"That stuff looks radioactive. What is it?"

Kenni grinned at Maizie's description. "It's Raylene's version of a margarita. I think we're gonna need it."

"What about Mrs. Hightower?"

"Raylene can finish her up. She owes me one, and that will keep both of them out of this conversation. I suspect the fewer people involved, the better."

Once they were settled with plastic cups of Raylene's brew, Maizie told her cousin everything. Including descriptions of her three new tennis outfits with the halter tops and plunging necklines.

When she finished, Kenni didn't say a word. It was hard to speak when your mouth was hanging open.

"Are you serious?" she finally choked out.

"Absolutely." Maizie placed her half-full cup on the low table in front of her. "I've tried sexy lingerie and romantic dinners." She threw up her hands. "I've even done a striptease and you know what he did? He said he was dead tired and could we do it later. Later!" Maizie's voice got louder with each word.

"Shh! Mrs. Hightower might be under the dryer, but I'm fairly sure people in the next county can hear you."

"Oh, okay." Maizie fell back in her chair.

"Let's look at this logically. Is there something going on at work that he hasn't told you? Maybe he's stressed—or he could really be tired. He loves you like crazy. Everyone can see that."

Clay hadn't said much about work lately and that was unusual.

"I'll make a deal with you," Kenni continued. "Go home, get dolled up, pull out all the stops on a romantic setting and ask him to take you away for the weekend. If that doesn't work, I'll reluctantly help you with this stupid scheme. What did Liza say?"

Maizie sighed. "She's on the same page you are. But all right. I'll give it my best shot."

CLAY WALKER HAD HAD a hell of a day. In point of fact, it had been a hellacious six months. The engineering contract his company had with a public/private partnership road project had gone south in too many ways to count.

The private development corporation had insisted on changes the department of transportation bureaucrats had vetoed, and vice versa. Consequently, construction was so far behind schedule it was impossible to catch up, and everyone was blaming his engineering firm. During this debacle, Clay had put out so many fires he felt like a wildfire jumper.

He should have listened to his gut. He'd been hesitant to bid on the project, but the temptation was too hard to resist. It was their way to the big time. Uh-huh. If things didn't improve soon their only option would be bankruptcy.

And then he had to add in the fact Maizie was making him nuts. They'd always gotten along so well, but lately it seemed she was constantly mad at him. He realized she wanted more attention, but he just didn't have it to give. There were only so many hours in the day, and his had been maxed to the hilt for months. God, what he wouldn't give for a week in the sun without emergencies and contentious situations.

Clay's current schedule had been a nightmare of meeting after meeting. Tonight all he wanted was a cold beer and a quiet evening of TV. But when he walked through the front door, Maizie met him in the living room. There were candles on the dining room table and soft music playing on the stereo.

Please, please, please—not tonight. Any other time—at least any time other than the last six months—Clay would have been randy and ready, but not now. Please God, not now. He was so tired he wouldn't be able to get it up even for the love of his wife.

Maizie was oblivious to his turmoil. But who could blame her? He hadn't been willing to share. Not only had she gone to a ton of trouble, she was absolutely gorgeous in an off-the-shoulder pale blue silk blouse. Normally he'd have that blouse off in thirty seconds. And a heartbeat later he'd have her in bed, but not tonight.

Clay could tell she was getting ready to say something important. He hoped that in his addled state he could come up with the right answer.

"Clay." Maizie put her arms around his neck. "I think we should go away for the weekend." She emphasized the suggestion with a sexy shimmer up and down his body.

Oh, sheesh! He pulled her into his arms and rested his chin on the top of her head. She was tall, but at 6'4" he still had a couple of inches on her.

"Maizie, sweetheart. I can't. There's nothing I'd love to do more than spend a weekend with you, preferably somewhere far away from telephones and e-mail and nasty clients. But right now it's impossible. I'm up to my ass in alligators on this project."

Clay was tempted to tell her about the precarious nature of their finances, but decided against it. He didn't want to worry her. Why should they both get ulcers? But even he knew that was a crock. The truth was he was embarrassed.

It was several seconds before Maizie pulled away, giving him a glance he couldn't quite decipher. If he was lucky she wouldn't be planning something nutty. But lately Lady Luck hadn't been smiling on him.

Chapter Seven

Maizie prided herself on excelling in almost every social situation. She could pull off a dinner party for twenty at the drop of a hat. Give her a couple of weeks and she could organize a formal ball. But being at home on a tennis court? Nope, that wasn't even vaguely in her repertoire.

"Mrs. Walker, I'm so glad you decided to join us."

Mrs. Walker? Was Clay's mother behind her? "Call me Maizie, please."

"Sure," Trip agreed before turning to the rest of the class. "Ladies, this is Maizie. Please make her feel at home."

She already knew many of the women—for the most part young matrons who lived in the new gated community. They were skinny, they were toned and she wasn't, not by a long shot.

She felt like a klutz. It'd been a long time since she'd played tennis in high school, so Maizie had started off with a beginner class, and it was a darned good thing. No matter how hard she tried, she couldn't get the stupid ball over the net.

To make matters worse, Maizie had long since passed the glowing stage. Even though it was a gorgeous autumn day, and not all that hot, she was sweating like a pig. Now *that* was a real turn-on.

Maizie hit an errant ball that pinged off the net before bouncing out of the court. This game was obviously not her bag, and she'd better improve— PDQ—or there would be a whole bunch of new tennis stuff for the next garage sale. Of all the schemes she'd concocted this one had to be the most ridiculous. And to be truthful, the chances of it working were almost nonexistent.

"Don't worry. You'll get better," Trip assured her.

"I'm not so sure about that," Maizie said with a chuckle. Everyone else had wandered off to the clubhouse in search of a cold drink.

"You're doing fine. Just keep trying."

That was easy for him to say. He could keep the ball inside the lines.

"Would you like some help gathering up the balls?" Maizie asked, wondering why the nubile young things hadn't stuck around. This was clearly a prime flirting opportunity.

"That would be great." Trip picked up one of the handled ball baskets that allowed for ball retrieval without bending over.

Maizie grabbed a ball sweeper that resembled a toy pop-up vacuum cleaner and went about corralling the tennis balls that littered the court. The pros made the game look easy, but the same could be said for gymnastics and ice skating. So even if her flirting idea was a bust, it might be fun to actually learn to play.

CLAY REALIZED HE WAS FRESH out of ideas about Maizie, so he decided to call in the cavalry—aka Liza and Kenni. He'd had to resort to cajoling and a smidgen of begging before they agreed to meet him at the Coffee Cup, a café at the opposite end of town from Miss Scarlett's Boudoir.

Clay's stomach was flip-flopping like a D.C. politician, so coffee was out of the question. What was the name of that tea Eleanor loved? Earl Grey—that was it. He ordered a cup and was about to take his first sip when his wife's sister and cousin strolled in.

"Over here," Clay said, trying to sound casual but failing miserably. The rumor mill in Magnolia Bluffs was remarkably efficient, and Maizie would have a fit if she heard they were meeting behind her back.

"What can I get you ladies?"

"A small latté for me," Kenni said.

"Make that two," Liza agreed.

To an uninvolved observer this would be nothing more than a coffee date with friends, but appearances could sometimes be deceiving. It didn't escape Clay's notice that as soon as he walked off, Liza and Kenni put their heads together for a private conversation.

"Here you go," Clay said when he returned with the drinks. The ladies were obviously not discussing the church social or even the price of tea in Timbuktu.

"So, what do you think?" he asked.

Liza took a deep breath. "We really can't tell you anything. I would if I could, honestly. But I can't."

"Can't or won't?"

"A little of both." She glanced at Kenni who nodded in agreement.

Clay rested his head on his fist. "Look, I'm not

asking you to betray a confidence. I simply need some help. She seems angry with me all the time and I don't know how to fix it. I don't know what's wrong." He held his hands up in supplication. "I'm desperate."

Liza rubbed the back of her neck. "Why don't you tell us what you think the problem is. Maybe we can help you without really helping you, if you see what I mean." Wink, wink.

Clay nodded. "Fair enough. I suspect there are a couple of things going on. First off, I think when Hannah moved out she started feeling unfulfilled. But she doesn't want to admit it. You know Maizie, she's always pooh-poohed the empty-nest idea."

Kenni spoke up. "That's a start, and for what it's worth I agree with you. So we have an empty nest, what else?"

Clay couldn't meet their eyes. "She wants me to spend more time with her."

"What's so hard about that?" Liza asked.

He sighed. "Maizie doesn't know this, so you can't tell a soul. Do I have your word?"

Although Kenni grimaced, she nodded. Liza followed suit.

"Our firm is in financial trouble. We won a contract that's now in the middle of a huge crisis. We're working on that new overpass on the interstate and the moron we're dealing with at the Department of Transportation has required more change orders than we can deliver. Alter this, move that, do that—nope, that's not right, try again. It's been one thing after another. Frankly, I think he's trying to tube the project. Consequently, the construction company has gone into a penalty phase and is about to go belly-up. If that happens, we don't get paid. And we've spent well over six months on the project." Clay massaged his temples. "After I've spent all day putting out fires, I'm too beat to do anything but fall into bed."

"There goes my advice." Liza huffed out a breath. "How about you?" she asked Kenni.

"Uh, me, too."

Liza took Clay's hand. "You need to tell Maizie what's happening. She really, really needs to know."

"I've waited too long. She's going to be so pissed that I didn't come to her right away. And to be completely honest, I'm humiliated that I let things get this out of hand."

"Oh, boy." Kenni took a deep breath. "You are in such trouble, and you're going to get in even deeper if you don't do something."

"I know. So how do we fix it?"

"We?" Liza asked.

"Please, please, please. I need your help." Clay wasn't above begging.

"How about this—Kenni and I'll discuss the situation and get back to you later."

"It's not perfect but I can work with it."

LIZA WALKED KENNI TO her car. "What do you suggest we do?"

Kenni hit the button on her remote but didn't open the door. "I'm afraid they're on a slippery slope. Considering how much they love each other, we have to help them straighten out this mess."

"As much as I hate to say it, I agree," Liza twirled her keys. "Personally, I'd like to smack them both."

"I'm with you on that one." Kenni hopped in her car, gave a saucy wave and backed out.

Liza watched as her cousin drove away. Things were going so well in her own life it made her feel guilty to see Maizie so unhappy. And if there was anything she could do to help, she was game.

Unfortunately, Liza was fresh out of ideas.

Chapter Eight

That night, Clay couldn't sleep. Sometime after midnight he decided to lay his cards on the table and take his knocks. Things couldn't get much worse. Could they?

He'd been up for hours trying to formulate a plan that would minimize the damage, but so far he had zilch. The sun was about to make an appearance before he settled on pampering.

"Wake up, sleepyhead," Clay said, sitting down on the side of the bed and waving a cup of coffee under Maizie's nose. "I have bear claws and apple fritters." Clay shook the pastry sack.

Maizie cracked an eye. "Is that for me?" she asked. "Please say it's mine."

"It certainly is." Clay set the cup on the bedside table and leaned over to give her a kiss. "Cute hair." He tugged on a curl and let it spring back into place. "We need to talk."

Maizie pulled herself up to a sitting position. "Do you mind if I have a shot of caffeine and a bite of sugar first?"

The question was obviously rhetorical, but it gave

him some breathing room. When had he become such a coward?

"This is so yummy," Maizie said as she took her first bite of apple fritter. "Considering you made a predawn trip to the bakery, and you made coffee, I have to wonder what you've been up to."

"Me?" He wished she didn't know him so well. "Uh…"

Clay was working up the courage to spill his guts when the phone rang. His first reaction was relief; his second was panic. Who would be calling at six a.m.?

Maizie grabbed the phone to check the Caller ID. "It's Hannah," she said before answering the call.

"What's wrong, baby?" The tension in Maizie's voice was almost palpable. Then she smiled and gave Clay a reassuring nod. "I'm sure he didn't mean it," she said before settling back against the pillows.

Clay took the interruption as a sign. Cluck, cluck, cluck, Chicken that he was, he decided to head to the office. "I'm going to work," he whispered.

"Hannah, hold on a second. Your daddy's leaving and I want to speak to him." Maizie held the phone against her chest and mouthed. "It's about her boy-friend. What did you want to talk about?"

"We can do it later. Let's go out to dinner tonight. We'll have a nice long chat then. What do you have going today?"

"I don't think I told you this but I've started taking tennis lessons at the club."

"Tennis?"

"I figured I needed the exercise and that sounded like a good way to get it. Bambi doesn't have school, so she can work and I'm going to play."

Clay shrugged. Maizie sweating? It was hard to imagine.

"Have a good time." He gave her a kiss and a wave before strolling out the door.

"I'm back." Maizie got comfortable for a long talk with her daughter. "So what did he say?"

THE BEGINNER CLASSES AT the club were available for drop-ins. At times there were too many students for the pro to handle. But on occasion there were so few students it was almost like having a private lesson. That was the situation Maizie encountered when she arrived at the club later that morning.

"Hi, Maizie. I didn't know you were available on weekdays." As usual, Trip Fitzgerald was drop-dead handsome in his crisp white shorts and dazzling polo.

"Normally I'm working but my assistant manager is covering for me. You remember PJ, don't you?"

"I do indeed. She's quite the saleswoman." Trip laughed. "Mom appreciated my shopping spree."

"PJ's one of a kind. I couldn't run the shop without her," Maizie said, then changed topic. "I realize I'm a terrible tennis player, but do you think there's any hope for me?"

Trip patted her shoulder. "Of course there is. You're a good athlete. You're just a little rusty."

Who was he kidding? Rusty didn't begin to describe her—totally oxidized would be more appropriate. But now that she'd started on this tennis venture, she was eager to learn.

"Okay, ladies, let's get ready to run," Trip announced with a maniacal gleam in his eye.

The two other ladies in the class were both well under thirty. Why couldn't she be content to "sweat to the oldies"?

Trip set up a serving machine and had them hitting ball after ball—forehands, backhands, overheads and volleys.

"Turn, step into the shot, watch the ball, follow through." If Trip said that once, he said it a dozen times. "Ladies, it's a backhand. That means it's coming from the other side. Turn, step into it. Watch the ball!"

His tirade was usually followed by her favorite. "Get your butt in gear! This ain't no sewing circle. I want to see some per-*spi*-ration. Ya hear me. Run. Get it going."

She had to wonder whether teaching a bunch of klutzes had driven him around the bend.

"Mrs. Walker, don't swat at the ball. Bring your racket back and get prepared as soon as it comes toward you. Once it bounces it's too late."

Maizie took a deep breath before she put her hands on her hips. Sweat was dripping from every pore. Glowing— get real. Even her socks were soaking. "I told you before. Call me Maizie. You're making me feel ancient."

He had the temerity to laugh. "Yes, ma'am. Uh, Maizie. You're not ancient, believe me." He tapped her on the bum with his tennis racket.

What was that about?

The lesson had lasted only an hour, but it was the longest sixty minutes in history. Maizie felt as if she'd been through the wringer. She used her arm to wipe the per-*spi*-ration off her face. Mama would absolutely die if she saw her. Maizie was so busy burrowing through her bag for a towel she didn't hear Trip walk up.

"Have you considered taking some semiprivate lessons, or perhaps even a private? I think you have potential."

She wasn't sure if this was Trip's version of marketing or whether he was telling the truth. But either way, she'd played along. It worked just fine for her own purposes, too.

"Is there someone who could do a private lesson with me tomorrow?" It wouldn't hurt to have PJ run the shop again. She'd appreciate the bonus and Maizie would love one more day without dealing with people like Jeannine Crabtree. And if Trip could teach her, so much the better.

"I'm available. Do you prefer morning or afternoon?"

"Any time is good."

"Why don't we go back to the office? I'll check the appointment book."

Maizie tossed the racket into her sports duffel and followed him across the court to the sports complex.

"I'm dying of thirst. How about you?" Trip asked as they passed an outdoor snack kiosk.

She'd glowed so much she probably didn't have a drop of moisture left in her system. "I'm pretty sure I'm dehydrated."

"I'll buy you a Coke."

"Thanks."

Thirty minutes later, Trip glanced at his watch. "As much as I've enjoyed this, we need to scoot on over to the office to set up your lesson."

"I'm sorry I've kept you." During their conversation Maizie had discovered they were close to the same age and amazingly they enjoyed many of the same things and even had some mutual acquaintances. Making a new friend was like scoring a great bargain—it was a ton of fun. And then there was always the jealousy angle.

Chapter Nine

That was the start of Maizie's obsession with tennis. If she wasn't at the boutique, she was on the court. Maizie took group lessons, semiprivate lessons and even a couple of privates. She was fixated on serves, volleys, approach shots and lobs, and she did them over and over again.

Following almost every lesson she'd head over to the club for a soft drink. It was a great way to meet some of the newcomers to Magnolia Bluffs, and Trip almost always joined the party. He was funny, charming and delightful to be around.

Clay didn't understand any of it, Liza said she was being obsessive and PJ was getting irritated. She didn't appreciate the fact her boss was AWOL more often than not.

Maizie couldn't explain her new passion, other than it made her feel young and competitive. She was toning up, getting a killer tan and had made a great new friend in Trip.

Occasionally she wondered what Clay had wanted to talk to her about. For some reason that escaped her

memory, they hadn't been able to make it to dinner.
And after that one incident he'd withdrawn so much
that now she wasn't sure she wanted to know.

In this case, however, ignorance *wasn't* bliss. If they
were going to save their marriage, they both had to
come clean. By gosh, if he was having an affair she'd
make him rue the day he was born. But truthfully she
couldn't imagine Clay philandering.

For her part, Maizie realized the jealousy scheme
would never have worked anyway. Clay wasn't around
enough to know if someone was flirting with her.
Looking back on it, Maizie now acknowledged it had
been a *really* bad idea.

EVERYTHING—AT LEAST THE professional side of her
life—came to a head almost two weeks into her in-
tense lessons. Maizie had just arrived at the boutique
when PJ confronted her about the tennis absences.
That's when Maizie decided she had to focus on her
business and her marriage. She'd been a selfish twit,
but no more. The fun was over. It was time to grow
up, and to prove it she canceled all her upcoming
lessons.

Maizie was busy patting herself on the back when
the phone rang.

"You're one hard chick to track down." Liza didn't
mince words.

"And hello to you, too."

"Kenni and I will be there in ten minutes. We wanted
to take you to lunch but with your tennis lessons, and
work and whatever, we haven't had any luck getting
hold of you."

Maizie hated to spoil Liza's tirade so she didn't bother to beg off. "I'm here, so come on over."

TEN MINUTES LATER LIZA and Kenni marched into Miss Scarlett's like a couple of avenging angels. PJ took one look at them and skedaddled off for a break. "I'm going to lunch." She grabbed her purse and was out the door in a flash.

"I think we need chocolate," Liza announced. "Are you using the same hiding place for the good stuff?"

Oh, this was going to be fun. "Yep, third cabinet from the left, top shelf."

Kenni made herself at home on the fainting couch.

Maizie sat down with her cousin. "So, what's the emergency?"

"We, uh, we wanted to—"

"We're here for an intervention." Liza tossed a bag of Lindt truffles on the table.

Maizie hadn't seen that one coming. "An intervention? What are you nitwits talking about? I'm not an alcoholic."

"No, but you're making a huge mistake and we refuse to sit back and let you ruin your marriage," Kenni said.

Liza popped a chocolate in her mouth. "Hence, the intervention."

"Why do you think I'm ruining my marriage?"

Kenni glanced at Liza before speaking. "We think your idea to make Clay jealous is dangerous. You have to stop it."

At first Maizie was flabbergasted, then she found it funny. "Have I told you guys that I love you?"

"Not lately," Liza said. "And I'm not sure what that has to do with anything."

"I'm trying to tell you that I already ditched my idea to make Clay jealous. It was dumb."

"I can't argue with that," Liza agreed. "So if you're not trying to get Clay's attention, what's with all the tennis?"

Maizie shot her twin her best "duh" look. "I'm playing tennis because it makes me feel good. They're called exercise-induced endorphins."

Kenni snorted. "Exercise-induced endorphins? Holy smoke. Who are you and what did you do with my cousin?"

"Yeah, where's my sister?"

"Stuff it, both of you. Hand over the chocolate," Maizie said, grabbing the bag of Swiss candy. "Besides, I've already decided to cut back on my tennis time. I'll admit it, I've become obsessed, and I've been neglecting my other obligations, but no more."

Chapter Ten

Several hours later Maizie was straightening the racks when the bell over the door jangled. She was expecting PJ to return from an errand so she didn't bother to look up.

"Would you watch the front while I go unpack our new inventory?" she asked.

"Are you going to pay me?" The voice was male and very familiar. It should be—she'd spent almost every day for the past two weeks with him.

"Hey, Trip. What can I do for you?"

The tennis pro leaned against the counter. "I thought I'd drop by to see if the rumor was true. Have you really cancelled all your lessons?"

"Sorry, it's true." Maizie shrugged. "I decided I needed to spend more time on my real job, especially since I probably won't make the pro tour."

"Yeah, there is that," he agreed, not bothering to hide his grin. "Think of it this way, you're getting a lot of vitamin D. What's more important than that?"

"Sometimes you have to make priorities, and unfortunately this is one of those occasions."

"Do you think you might come back in the future?"

"Maybe later," Maizie said with a laugh. "PJ wasn't happy about my being gone so much. And I can't afford to irritate her—she's indispensible. So there went the tennis, at least for now."

"That's too bad."

"Yeah, it is. I really enjoyed the lessons, even if you did make me sweat." And even if she was a middle-aged woman with melting makeup in a bevy of hot young things half her age.

"Did you come in to see me or are you on another shopping expedition?" Maizie realized that sounded flirtatious, which she was supposed to be avoiding, but it didn't mean a thing. Flirting was in her blood.

Trip made a show of smacking his forehead. "Oh, right. I need a present for, uh, my mother."

"What's the occasion?" Maizie asked. "The last time you were here you were buying her a birthday present."

"What can I say? I'm a good son. She's going on a cruise and I thought I'd send her a bon voyage gift."

Although Maizie didn't quite believe him, she never turned away a paying customer. "Is there anything she needs?"

"Who?"

"Your mother."

"I don't know. Why don't you just show me some things, and then let me take you to lunch?"

"Sure, why not?" She went out to eat with friends all the time. "PJ will be back shortly. In the meantime we can give that credit card of yours a workout."

CLAY WASN'T PARTICULARLY HUNGRY but his partner Harvey Tucker was craving deep-fried onion rings. That's how they ended up in the dimly lit dining room of the Dixie Draught, Magnolia Bluffs' only brew pub.

"Is that Maizie back there?" Harvey asked, peering into the gloomy recesses of the bar. "And who's she with?"

"Where?"

"That way." He indicated a booth at the rear of the restaurant. When Clay's eyes adjusted, he realized Harv was right. That was Maizie, but who was the dude? No time like the present to find out. He walked purposefully toward them, Harv trailing in his wake.

"You don't mind if we join you, do you?" Clay asked his wife, not giving her a chance to answer before he squeezed into the booth next to her.

"I'm Maizie's husband, Clay Walker. And you are?" The question was more of a demand than a request. Clay knew he was being rude, but after spying his wife in a tête-à-tête with a handsome stranger, he simply didn't care.

"Harv, sit down. We're going to join my wife and her friend." Although his partner looked as if he'd rather dine with terrorists, he reluctantly complied.

"Clay!" Maizie jabbed him in the side with her elbow. "Be nice. This is my tennis coach, Trip Fitzgerald. And, Trip, this jerk is my husband."

"Glad to meet you," Trip said with a smile.

"Yeah, you, too."

What else could Clay say? He was so jealous he couldn't see straight. That was the reason he'd messed up royally. God, he was afraid he was losing his wife.

Chapter Eleven

Ever since the fiasco in the brew pub the atmosphere in the Walker household had been so tense you could cut it with a knife. Yes, Clay was jealous, but the reality wasn't as thrilling as Maizie had imagined when she started her stupid scheme. And thanks to Mama they were now unwilling participants in a country club fund-raiser.

"When can we go home?" Clay whispered.

"We can leave after the auction. I donated a makeover and I want to see who wins it."

Clay pulled on his collar as if it was choking him. "Okay," he reluctantly agreed.

"Stop that." Maizie swatted her husband's hand. The man cleaned up quite nicely. In fact, he was absolutely gorgeous in his charcoal suit with the crisp white shirt and silk tie. Actually in his normal attire of faded jeans and chambray shirt he was mighty fine, too. It was a shame she was still to mad at him to tell him so.

"You know how I hate these dress-up things," he groused.

Maizie opened her mouth for a rebuke when someone ran a finger down her bare back.

"What—" It took a couple of seconds to process what was happening and another heartbeat to think, "Oh, crap."

Maizie turned so fast she smacked Clay with her purse. "Trip, what are you doing here?"

"I work—"

"Get your hands off my wife, pretty boy." Clay pushed Maizie aside to confront Trip.

"Stop it!" The last thing Maizie needed was a brawl at the country club. Mama would have a fit.

Though Trip briefly looked taken aback he quickly recovered. "Mr. Walker, it's nice seeing you again." The words were appropriate though the tone was definitely sarcastic.

"Maizie, I hope to see you back in class soon." He flashed her a toothpaste-white smile before strolling off.

"What was that all about?" Clay demanded. "He had his hands all over you. Do you have something going on with him?"

"What do you mean, 'Going on with him'? Are you accusing me of cheating?" Maizie jabbed a finger at Clay's chest. Smoke was about ready to spew from her ears.

"He teaches tennis. Nothing more. I like taking lessons. That's why I bought all those new outfits." Maizie slammed her hands on her hips and gave him the "don't mess with me" look that meant he was in major trouble.

Clay knew he was skating on thin ice, but jealousy had obliterated all common sense.

"What outfits? We're not discussing clothes, we're talking about some smarmy twit touching you." As soon as the words were out of his mouth he knew he'd made a huge mistake.

"What outfits? What outfits! The ones with the short skirts and halter tops. The ones where my boobies hang out for everyone to see." Maizie gestured graphically toward her breasts. "You remember these, don't you?"

The pitch of her voice went up with every sentence until she was doing a great Betty Boop imitation.

Clay grabbed her hand and pulled her toward the exit. "People are listening," he hissed. If Maizie wanted to have a knock-down, drag-out fight, fine. But there was no way in hell he'd do it in front of half the town. The rose garden was probably deserted so that would have to do.

"Would you mind telling me what that was all about?" he asked once they were away from the main building. Although Clay was trying to be patient, he was almost at his wits' end.

Maizie glared at him. "You don't pay any attention to me. I can dress up, or I can dress down, or I can get buck naked and nothing makes any difference. How *do* I get your attention?"

Clay sighed. "How about acting like a grown-up instead of a spoiled brat?" Oh, brilliant. Sleep deprivation had turned him into the village idiot.

Initially, Maizie was speechless. But then she started stammering and turned bright red.

Crap!

"Look." Clay took a deep breath. This wasn't the best time to tell her about their financial situation but better late than never.

"Our company is on the verge of going belly-up. All

I've been able to think about lately is how to save our rear ends."

Maizie didn't utter a word. She didn't have to; her face said it all. At least she wasn't screaming.

"We realized that doing the engineering for the highway was almost too big for us to handle, but we bid on it anyway. In the past six months we've had problems with the state, the county and the contractor. As a result of all the confusion and the planned slow downs, we haven't been paid by the contractor in months. And we won't be anytime soon."

Clay had assumed Maizie would be sympathetic, or at the very least understanding.

"You dolt! Why didn't you tell me? You were going through something like that and you didn't let me know? I'm your wife," she screeched. "We're supposed to share everything. Everything!"

Clay almost expected her to deck him. Why was *she* getting all frothed up? He was the injured party, wasn't he?

"Calm down and I'll explain."

But Maizie wasn't ready to listen. She closed her eyes to tune him out. "I don't think I want you in my house right now. Wait, change that to I know I don't want to see you in my bed." Even though she made the announcement quietly, Clay could sense the fiery volcano bubbling beneath the surface.

That did it. "Fine. If that's how you feel about it, that's just peachy. I'll find someone to take you home."

"Fine!" She stomped her foot. "Don't bother to come by for your stuff because it'll be gone. Do you hear me? Gone, goodbye, adios."

"You'd better not do anything with my things. If you don't want to live with me, that's great, but don't mess with my possessions."

"What valuable possessions, your Little League trophy?"

"Yeah, my Little League trophy." Clay stepped back to take a deep breath.

"I'm leaving." He had to get out of there before he said something they couldn't recover from. They'd gone from okay to catastrophic in two point two seconds. How had it happened? And even more important, where did they go from here?

Chapter Twelve

Maizie didn't know how long she'd been sitting on the concrete bench before Liza appeared. She'd ruined everything. When was she going to learn to control her temper?

"What's going on out here?" Liza asked as she put an arm around Maizie's shoulders.

That did it. Maizie broke into sobs. "I've made such a mess of things," she wailed, punctuating the flood of tears with a series of hiccups.

"Honey, what happened?"

"Clay and I had a huge fight. He walked off and left me here."

"A fight? Is that all?"

Maizie shook her head. "I told him I didn't trust him and I didn't want to live with him."

"Good gravy! Why would you say that?"

Maizie explained as much about the fight as she could. It was almost like childbirth—it couldn't be explained and shouldn't be remembered.

"Is that why he wanted me to take you home?"

"I suppose so. Did he say where he was going?"

Maizie sniffed. Darn! Her nose was running like a faucet and she didn't have a tissue or a sleeve. When things went bad, they went bad in a big way.

"Let's take the back exit," Liza suggested. "You have raccoon eyes and your face is all red and puffy. If anyone sees you like this, you'll be the talk of the town."

"Okay, let's go. I'm sure Clay will be home when I get there."

But not only was Clay gone when they arrived, so was his car, his golf clubs and most of his clothes. Where was he?

Liza gave Maizie a pitying look as they went back to the kitchen following a full house inspection.

"What?"

"Honey, I hate to tell you this, but he's not coming back. At least not tonight. Do you want me to stay here with you?"

"What would Zack say?"

Liza pulled out her cell phone. "Let me see."

"Please don't. I'll be okay." Not really, but at her age did she want a baby-sitter?

"Zack, honey," Liza said into her phone, "I'm going to spend the night with Maizie."

There was a lengthy silence on Liza's end of the line. "I'll tell you all about it when I get home. I love you."

After she disconnected she went to the refrigerator. "Where's the wine? We're going to have a slumber party. Then we'll come up with a solution for this fiasco."

The twins worked their way through two bottles of wine, a bowl of popcorn, a plate of nachos and a pan of brownies before Liza had an epiphany.

"You're going to court him! He's jealous. That's

good. It means he loves you. So make him feel like the most special man in the world. Take him out to dinner, then to the movies and end up at the old necking spot. Approach this as if you were seventeen again."

"How am I going to do that when I don't even know where he is?" This time Maizie's hiccup was courtesy of too much wine.

"You leave that to me. I have connections with the local cops." Liza giggled. "Did you know I have an intimate relationship with the sheriff?"

"Yep, I got that." Maizie yawned. "I think I'd better hit the sheets. I'm already going to have the mother of all headaches in the morning."

IT WAS AFTER TEN BEFORE Maizie finally managed to open her eyes. Her head was pounding and her mouth was as dry as the Mojave Desert. If there was a God in the heavens, Liza wouldn't be faring any better.

Maizie slowly put one foot in front of the other until she finally stumbled into the kitchen in search of a Coke and some saltines. She was rubbing the icy can on her throbbing forehead when Liza wandered in. Little Miss Sunshine was talking on her cell.

"Who told you?" Liza pointed at the can and then the refrigerator.

Maizie knew exactly what she wanted—salvation in the form of sugar and caffeine.

"Do you know how long he plans to be there?" Liza popped the top on the Coke and slugged back a huge drink.

"I'll be home shortly. Okay, see you soon." She disconnected and immediately grabbed a cracker.

"You're not going to believe this."

"What?" Maizie was expecting to hear that her husband was camped out at the extended stay motel on the highway.

"Clay's moved into Mama and Daddy's garage apartment."

"He's done what?" That was the last place she would've expected him to go.

"He saw Daddy as he was leaving the country club last night and our father invited him to move in." Liza was apparently having a hard time believing it, too.

"So where do I go from here? My husband has left me and my father is in collusion with the jerk."

"I still think we have a solid plan."

"Why don't you give me the details again?" Maizie was a wee bit fuzzy about last night.

"You're going to court him, remember?"

"Oh, yeah." Maizie wasn't quite sure she had agreed, but she had a vague memory of the discussion.

TWO DAYS LATER MAIZIE still hadn't heard from her errant sweetie. She could call him, of course, but he was the one who had moved out. Shouldn't he make the first move?

Damn it! Maizie was sipping her third cup of coffee and working up a big mad. If Clay thought she would be sitting here when he was ready, he was sadly mistaken. As for the rest of his stuff, well, she knew what to do with that! There was a perfectly good curb just waiting for it.

Intellectually, Maizie realized she was making a huge mistake. She simply couldn't help herself. It was a caffeine-induced psychosis, that's what it was.

Out went the baseball trophies—including the national Little League championship—the sports equipment, the treadmill—that one took some muscle—and the remainder of his clothes.

Maizie looked at the pile of her husband's belongings and slapped her hands together. The feeling of satisfaction lasted until she broke into tears and ran back to the house as if Cujo was nipping at her heels.

Several cars slowed and a couple even stopped. They were obviously trolling for free stuff. Free stuff—where did they get that idea? Was there a sign out there saying *Take Me?* Of course not. Mama would have a fit.

Maizie grabbed her cell and ran out to shoo away the vultures. A guy in a baggy pair of pants and a faded wife beater had a pair of Clay's jeans in his hand. Not that his fat rear would ever fit into those Wranglers.

"Get away from my husband's clothes."

"Lady, someone put this stuff out for the garbage." He gave her a dirty look before hocking a loogie at her feet.

Gag.

"That's not trash. My husband's coming to pick it up." Maizie held up her phone hoping to scare him off. "I'm calling the cops."

What do you know—it worked. She wouldn't be surprised if the guy was wanted by the police. When the redneck jumped into his Camaro and hit the gas, gravel sprayed everywhere.

Maizie was congratulating herself when she spied something lying by the curb. It was metal, it was mangled and it was Clay's Little League trophy.

Oh, dear Lord. He'd never forgive her.

She bent over to pick up the pieces. "Thanks, buddy," she muttered.

Maizie punched in Clay's office number. *Please, please, please answer the phone.*

"Clay Walker."

She was at a loss for words. How was she going to explain this? "Uh, Clay. I put your stuff out on the curb and some people have already tried to take things."

She didn't want him to lose all that sporting equipment. "I stopped them but you need to get over here right away. I have to go to work."

There was such a long pause Maizie was afraid they'd been disconnected.

"You did what?" He said it so softly she almost didn't hear him.

"Your things are on the lawn and some people have already stopped to rummage through them."

"I thought that's what you said." He hung up without another word.

Well, crumb! Maizie stared at the phone, expecting it to ring. Ten minutes later Clay roared up in his pickup. Without even glancing at the house, he tossed his belongings in the vehicle, muttering the entire time. Maizie couldn't hear what he was saying but certain words were easy to lip-read.

Chapter Thirteen

Mama was driving Maizie nuts. The woman had called at least a thousand times over the weekend, but thanks to Caller ID Maizie had been able to dodge a barrage of maternal advice. Now that it was Monday all bets were off. Sure as shootin' her mom would show up at the Boudoir.

"Mother alert. She's coming down the sidewalk." Maizie had clued PJ in on the mess she called her private life. "Do you want to hide? I'll make an excuse for you."

"Thanks, but no. I'll have to face her sooner or later." It was hard not to think of her mom as a traitor. How dare her parents take Clay's side!

"Hi, Mama. What brings you to town?" Maizie asked when her mother walked in. She was determined to be polite, even if it killed her.

"Good morning, PJ. How's your family?" Mama ignored Maizie's question.

So that's how the game was going to be played.

"The girls are growing like weeds. Thanks for asking, ma'am," PJ said. "Hey, Maze. I'm going to the back to steam some of that new inventory. Give a yell if you need me."

Thanks a ton, friend. "I'll do that." Maizie braced herself for a serious discussion with her mother.

"What is my son-in-law doing camped out in my garage apartment? I love him dearly, but he needs to be at home in his own bed." She gave Maizie her best "Mother's not pleased" combo of folded arms and steely-eyed glare. Mama had a frown that could scare a Navy SEAL into submission.

"I don't know," Maizie answered. She wasn't about to discuss her marital problems—or her lack of a sex life—with her *mother*.

Her resolve lasted until Eleanor Westerfield intensified her glower. Lordy, the woman could give the CIA lessons. Then when Eleanor picked up Maizie's hand and started drawing little circles on her palm, she broke.

"We had a fight and it went from bad to worse. The reason he's at your house is that I told him I didn't want to live with him anymore. And—" God, she hated to say this "—this morning I tossed his stuff out on the curb."

Mama rubbed her forehead. That was never a good sign. "Mary Stuart, how could you do that? Clay loves you like crazy and let me tell you, he's miserable."

"Mama, he didn't tell me his company is in financial trouble. He kept something that important from me." She sniffed, trying to unsuccessfully hold back a deluge of tears. "We're supposed to share everything. He left me out!" she wailed.

Although Eleanor was a good five inches shorter

than her daughter, she managed to pull Maizie into her arms.

"Honey, men do that. He didn't want to worry you. It's a throwback to the old-fashioned idea that women need to be protected, and he's a Southerner. That's what Southern men do."

Maizie's head was telling her that Mama was right. Her heart was saying something entirely different.

"So what are we going to do about this?" Mama asked.

It wasn't good when Mama used "we," especially when she was discussing a plan.

"Don't look at me like that, Missy. He can't live over my garage forever." Eleanor threw up her hands. "I love cooking for him, but he's eating us out of house and home."

"You're feeding him?"

"Breakfast and dinner."

"No wonder he hasn't come back. You're the best cook in town."

In Eleanor Westerfield's world that was the ulti-mate compliment. Unfortunately, it didn't deter her from her goal.

"So what are we going to do?" she repeated.

"Liza thinks I should court him. Wine, dine and date."

Mama cocked her head, obviously considering the situation. "That's brilliant! It's certainly not something he going to expect. So when do you get started?"

"I don't know." Maizie didn't bother to tell her they had come up with that idea over two bottles of wine and enough chocolate to give a monk the giggles.

"The sooner the better, I say. But first you have to forgive him. And that has to come from the heart, where it matters."

"I think I need forgiveness as much as he does. I'm still mad at him for keeping secrets, but I have to admit I'm at least partially responsible for this fiasco." Maizie gave a sheepish shrug. "He accused me of acting like a spoiled brat, and as embarrassing as it is, I have to say he's right."

"There is that," Mama agreed.

"I'll call Liza and Kenni to set up at time to meet." She looked as if she wanted to clap her hands in glee. "We'll come up with a plan."

Her mother was getting into the spirit of things, and as dearly as Maizie loved her mom, she could be a steamroller.

"A gift would be a nice way to start." Without batting an eyelash, Eleanor went into her party-planner mode. "I think you should go for something masculine, with a message. That would be perfect."

So where was Maizie supposed to find this masculine gift with a magic message?

Where was that "never fail to please" personal shopper when she needed her?

Chapter Fourteen

Trina Carruthers had been Maizie's archenemy since the eighth grade. Just the thought of walking in her store gave Maizie heartburn, but considering that Trina's Emporium was the only place in town that made gift baskets, she didn't have a choice.

"C'n I help you?" The clerk popped her gum in time to the song playing on the radio.

"I'd like a basket done up in the University of Georgia colors with some cans of beer, a couple of boxes of popcorn, maybe a pom-pom or two. You know, that kind of thing. It's for my husband."

The clerk snapped her gum a few more times. "Is it for a special occasion?"

"No. I thought I'd surprise him."

"Okey-doke, just a minute." The clerk gave her gum another chomp before heading back to find her boss.

Maizie heard giggling and whispering before Trina deigned to show her ugly mug.

"Hey, Maize. I hear you want a basket with pom-poms and beer cans." Trina tried to hold back her laughter, but ended up snorting instead.

What was so funny?

"Uh-huh."

"That's not on our normal price list so let me figure it out." She took a pencil from behind her ear. "So, how's everything goin'?"

Had Trina heard about Clay leaving her?

"I'm doing okay." Maizie just wanted to get out of there.

"We can modify our normal UGA basket and make it the adult version. That'll be fifty bucks plus tax. Does that work for you?"

Was she kidding? "Yeah, that's great."

"Do you want it delivered?"

Her old nemesis was dying to know what was happening, but there was no way Maizie was giving her that ammunition.

"No. I'll pick it up." Information concerning her reconciliation project was strictly on a need-to-know basis. And Trina definitely didn't need to know.

"When will it be ready?"

"Day after tomorrow should do it."

"Great." Maizie handed over her credit card, glad to have taken the first step. She wasn't certain Liza's idea would work, but it was better than doing nothing. The fact that Clay hadn't called or e-mailed or anything was about to send her into a panic.

A fight like this was a once in a lifetime—please God! At least the make-up sex would be stupendous. If they ever got that far.

TWO DAYS LATER, MARY Stuart Walker found herself standing on the miniscule porch of her mother's garage apartment holding the most ridiculous basket she'd ever laid eyes on. The pom-poms were the size of basketballs, and there was enough beer to slake the thirst of a chain gang. A dozen beer cans were glued to dowels and nestled next to the pom-poms. It was redneck taste at its finest.

Did Trina still blame her for the quarterback and the prom debacle? Terrible as that was it wasn't completely her fault. That infamous escapade had occurred when she and Clay had decided to date other people.

Maizie knocked again, alternating between hoping Clay was home and praying he wasn't. Mostly the latter.

"Mary Stuart, what are you doing up there?"

Deep down she'd hoped to drop off the basket and avoid Mama, but Lady Luck was obviously missing in action.

Before she could answer, Mama was halfway up the stairs.

"*What* is that thing?" Mama eyed the basket. And why not? It was a nightmare.

"A gift. I brought it for Clay. Remember we discussed giving him a present."

Mama glanced back and forth between Maizie and the basket, and then broke into a belly laugh.

Eleanor Westerfield and a belly laugh? Would wonders never cease?

"I thought you were trying to make up with him, not encourage him to drink himself senseless. Leave that thing on the stoop and come for coffee." Mama started back down the stairs. "He went out with Zack and Win, so I don't suspect he'll be home anytime soon."

"Yes, ma'am." No matter how old you were, a parental demand required immediate attention.

Maizie put down the basket and followed her mother to the kitchen. The Westerfields' kitchen hadn't changed since the sixties—same appliances, same color scheme and the same pine table that had been the epicenter of the family for years.

"Please tell me you didn't pay money for that… abomination." She handed Maizie a steaming mug of coffee and put a plate of homemade chocolate-chip cookies on the table.

"I did," Maizie admitted. "Quite a bit in fact."

Mama refilled her own mug and joined her daughter. "Is it supposed to be a joke?"

"No, actually it isn't. I paid Trina Carruthers fifty bucks to put it together."

Eleanor gave an eloquent snort. "That girl's taste is all in her mouth. The only reason she's still in business is because folks don't have a choice."

"Yeah, it's pretty gross, isn't it? She really doesn't like me, so I suppose that didn't help."

"You never told me what she has against you." Mama cocked her head. "It started in high school, didn't it? What did you do?"

Maizie assumed an innocent, wide-eyed expression. "Me? Why would you think *I* did something?"

Mama didn't say a word. She didn't have to.

Maizie held her hands up. "Okay, I give. I sort of hijacked her boyfriend at the prom. It wasn't *all* my fault, really it wasn't. Ask Liza, she was there." She'd gone to the prom without a date and no one would ask her to dance because of Clay. So she took matters into

her own hands and asked Arlon Higgenbotham—
Trina's on-again, off-again boyfriend.

"Lordy, girl." Mama shook her head. "Oh, well,
that's water under the bridge. So back to the problem
at hand, do you have any plans for winning your
husband back, other than showering him with ugly
gifts?"

"Not really. I've left him a couple of messages."
More like hundreds, but who was counting? "And he
hasn't returned any of my calls."

Mama got up to freshen her coffee. "He's not too
happy with you, but I suspect he's more hurt than mad."

"So what do you suggest?" Maizie bit into another
cookie.

"I have an idea, but let's get your sister over here and
see what she thinks. In the meantime you can help me
with these pies for the bake sale."

Maizie had been so immersed in her own problems
she hadn't noticed the desserts in various stages of
completion. "What's the charity and how many did
you promise them?"

"Just ten and they're for the Humane Society."

"What do you want me to do?" Maizie rummaged
through the drawer looking for an apron. Baking wasn't
her forte but she was a good helper.

By the time Liza arrived Maizie was covered in flour
and had a smudge of blueberry pie filling on her face.

"You can't stay clean when you're cooking, can
you?" Liza asked, wiping blue goo off her sister's
cheek. "What's the big emergency? I was in the middle
of something."

"Something wicked, I hope." Lately Maizie had a

one-track mind. Just because she wasn't getting any didn't mean she couldn't live vicariously.

And Liza was a mind reader. "Nope, afraid not. We were raking leaves."

"Oh. You want a little of this." Maizie held up a spatula with the remnants of the chocolate pie filling.

"You go ahead. You probably need it more than I do."

Maizie saluted as she licked the plastic utensil. Liza was right. If she couldn't have love, by God she'd have chocolate.

Chapter Fifteen

As usual, Liza didn't mince words. "So why are we here?"

"I started my courting campaign and I'm afraid I've already hit a snag." Maizie joined her sister at the table.

"What's the problem?" Liza pulled the plate of chocolate-chip cookies closer and helped herself.

"I bought him a gift basket and left it on the porch."

"So?"

"Go take a gander," Mama chimed in. "It's the tackiest thing I've ever seen."

"You bought him something tacky?" Liza shot Maizie a "what's up" look. "I thought you were trying to get back in his good graces."

"I am." Maizie popped her with a dish towel. "Trina Carruthers had other ideas."

Liza hooted. "Don't tell me you bought something from Trina! You know better than that. She can't stand you. This I've got to see." Liza strolled over to peer out the window.

"You mean that red-and-black eyesore is supposed to be a present?" Her cackle was distinctly unlady-like.

"Stuff a sock in it." Maizie's demand resulted in another bout of laughter.

Liza finally managed to get herself under control—sort of. "Girl, we need to talk," she said, still shaking.

"That's why we called you, sister dearest," Maizie tried for sarcasm but failed miserably. "I need some help. I haven't dated anyone but Clay since the eighth grade. And yes, I know the whole jealousy thing was really, really stupid."

Liza didn't say a word. Her hug said it all. "We'll fix it. When we put our heads together we're damned formidable, aren't we Mama?"

Eleanor Westerfield gave her youngest daughter a high five. "We certainly are. We're Iron Magnolias."

"That's steel." Maizie winked at her twin.

"What?"

"Steel, we're Steel Magnolias.

"Whatever." Mama shrugged. "Steel, iron, it's all metal. The only thing that matters is that Maizie has stumbled onto something. Their marriage is based on humor." She looked from one daughter to the other. "Am I right?"

Maizie nodded. "You are."

"So, let's take advantage of that. If Clay doesn't find that beer basket funny, I'll be very surprised. So, in a couple of days I think you should send him something even more over the top."

"Hmm." Liza rested her head on her fists. "That could work. What do you think, Maze?"

Maizie thought she should step in front of a bus and put herself out of her misery.

"I've got it!" Liza exclaimed. Her legal profession

fooled a lot of people, but Maizie knew better. Liza was the ultimate instigator.

"What?" Eleanor seemed as eager as her lawyer daughter.

Liza snapped her finger. "Brenda Lee. What do you think?" Her grin couldn't possibly bode well.

"What about Brenda Lee?" Maizie couldn't help being suspicious.

"We'll hire someone to serenade him with Brenda's 'I'm Sorry' song. Every good country boy knows that tune. He won't be able to resist."

Swell. "This making-up thing is getting expensive."

"We'll all chip in, won't we, Mama?"

"Are you kidding? I want my garage apartment back," Eleanor agreed. "I'm on board."

"I'll take care of all the details," Liza said. "We'll do something every day until he gives in." She was getting way too enthusiastic. "Tonight we'll let him enjoy the basket. Tomorrow we'll see if we can round up an ersatz Brenda Lee. How does that sound?"

It sounded insane, but what did Maizie have to lose? "Okay, let's go for it." She wasn't convinced it would work, but things were so mucked up she'd take help from any source, even her crazy mother and her equally nutty sister.

CHAOTIC WAS ABOUT THE only way Clay could describe his life. There wasn't much he could do about the disaster at the office, but he could work on his marriage. And since talking to Kenni and Liza hadn't got him anywhere, he decided to get a male perspective from

Zack and Win. When Clay sent out an SOS they'd agreed to meet him at the Dixie Draught.

Zack shot him a look of sympathy once they were all seated and had beers in hand. "I hear you're living in Eleanor's garage apartment. That's too bad."

"I'd heard the rumors but I wasn't sure they were true." Win smiled broadly. "Why don't you fill us in?"

"It all started when the tennis pro started touching Maizie in front of me and I got all pissed off. It went downhill from there. I said things I shouldn't have said, and Maizie got even. She told me she didn't want to live with me anymore."

"That's cold." Win gave a mock shiver. "Do you really think there's something going on between Maizie and the tennis dude?"

"No. I overreacted."

"The shouting match at the country club has hit the rumor mill." Zack tossed in that bit of info.

"I was afraid of that." Clay glanced at Win. "But you're not in the loop, huh? Kenni hasn't said anything?"

"Nope, afraid not." Win called a waitress over. "Before we get too deep into this conversation I think I need some sustenance. How about you guys? You want some wings, or nachos or something?"

"Why don't you order up a couple of each? I'm sure we'll be here long enough to polish 'em off." Zack leaned back and crossed one booted foot on his knee. "So what are we missing?"

Leave it to a cop to get right to it.

"I messed up. I hadn't told Maizie that my company's in serious financial trouble and when she started ragging on me about not paying enough attention to her, I blurted it out."

"Bad move." Win grimaced in commiseration.

"Yeah, I know. So what do I do now?" Clay asked. "And even more important, is there something going on with the girls that I need to know about?"

Zack shook his head. "I have a feeling they're cooking up some kind of scheme, but honestly, I don't have any particulars."

"Can you get anything out of Liza?" Clay asked, even knowing Zack wouldn't betray his wife's trust. "Forget that. But I would appreciate any help you can give me. I'm sure you've heard about Maizie tossing everything I own out on the lawn." Clay frowned. "My national championship Little League trophy got broken. I worked my ten-year-old butt off to win that thing."

"Hey, man, that's too bad," Win sympathized. His compassion, however, didn't deter him from digging into the nachos.

"It's not right when a man's trophy gets busted," Zack agreed.

"So, back to what I can do."

"Do you love her?" Win asked, using his best courtroom interrogation skills.

"Absolutely."

"Are you miserable?" Zack asked.

"Yep, afraid so."

"Do you want to move out of Eleanor's garage?" Zack tried to make it a serious question, but spoiled it by chuckling.

"Are you kidding?"

Zack and Win shared a glance before Zack took charge of the conversation. "Considering we're working blind, I think your best bet is to hang tight and see what she does next. Then we can plan accordingly."

"I wouldn't wait too long, though," Win added. "That's a sure way to mess things up." He spoke from the experience of a trial lawyer.

"Wait, but not too long. How do I know what's too long?" Clay asked. "Do I wait a week? Longer?"

"Why don't you try for a week, and then if nothing has happened we can reconvene and discuss the next step," Zack suggested. Win nodded his agreement.

"I'm game. So you really think she'll try something soon?"

"I'd be surprised if she didn't," Zack said. "The Westerfield twins aren't known for their patience."

AN HOUR AND A HALF later Clay parked his Dodge king cab beside his in-laws' garage apartment. What was that on the porch?

Clay cut the engine and carefully mounted the stairs. What *was* that thing? Pom-poms? Beer cans? He started laughing and couldn't stop. Until the stink bomb went off.

That stench was unmistakable. Back in junior high Clay and a buddy set off a couple of those in the boys' restroom. Now, he kicked the basket off the porch in frustration. It was the best he could do until the smell dissipated.

So that's what she thought of him. Clay scrubbed his hand over his face. Damn! Instead of offering an apology, Maizie had launched a particularly odious volley.

This was war.

Chapter Sixteen

The Westerfield ladies had their noses pressed against the kitchen window eagerly awaiting Clay's reaction. There was a collective gasp when he deep-sixed the basket and stomped into the apartment.

"Why did he do that?" Liza was the first to speak.

Yeah, why had he done that? Maizie wondered. Sure it was ugly, but it was the thought that counted, right? Besides, it had cost her fifty bucks.

"I think I'll ask him exactly that." Eleanor jerked open the back door, allowing noxious fumes to waft in. "Good Lord, what is that smell?" She waved her hands in an attempt to ward off the smell that was vaguely reminiscent of a sewer treatment plant.

In unison Maizie and Liza exclaimed, "Trina Carruthers!"

Oh, man, *this* had turned into a debacle.

Mama slammed the door shut. "You two make yourselves scarce. I'm going to take care of this."

That scared Maizie spitless, but what other option did she have?

ELEANOR HELD HER NOSE as she tossed the basket into the side yard.

"Clayton dear, it's Eleanor," she yelled.

Clay had finally managed to calm down with the help of a cold beer and an inane television program. Right now the only thing he wanted to hear from his mother-in-law was an acknowledgment that her daughter was a certifiable lunatic.

He leaned over the railing and noticed she'd removed the evidence. "Hi, Eleanor, what can I do for you?"

"Have you had supper?" He didn't see that one coming.

"I had nachos at the Dixie Draught."

"Oh dear, that's not enough. Give me an hour and then get yourself on down here. I'm going to fry up a chicken."

"Yes, ma'am." It was a good thing he'd only had the one beer. He'd need to be stone sober to handle Eleanor.

Bennett Westerfield was at the kitchen table having a cup of coffee when Clay joined them. At best, he looked embarrassed. At worst, it appeared he was about to jump and run. Clay could relate.

"Hey, Bennett. What's up?"

Maizie's dad studied the contents of his cup. "Not much. How about you?"

"Life's kind of stinky." Clay was proud that he could say that with a straight face.

Bennett smiled. "That's what I hear."

Eleanor gave Clay a swat. "Sit down. I'm whipping up some potatoes."

Clay grabbed a drumstick from the platter Eleanor took from the warming oven, earning another smack in the process. Even under these circumstances, he was as comfortable in the Westerfields' kitchen as he was in his own.

"Here you go." Eleanor put a steaming plate of food in front of him and then sat down. "Bennett has something to tell you about Maizie's gift."

Clay's appetite disappeared. "She made it perfectly clear what she thinks of me."

"This whole thing is a disaster. Not that it hasn't had help from some folks who should know better." Bennett shot his wife a telling look. "Maizie's trying to make up with you. That's was what the basket was all about. Unfortunately things got a little messed up."

"Messed up?" That was a bit of an understatement.

"My baby girl bought that basket from Trina Carruthers and Trina's not exactly fond of our daughter. I called her to see what she had to say."

It was hard for Clay to think of his voluptuous Maizie as anyone's baby girl, but he decided he'd better skip over that one.

"What did she say?" Clay had never known Trina well, but he was aware of the tension between her and Maizie, and it all went back to the prom.

"At first she didn't want to talk to me, but I convinced her otherwise." Bennett chuckled. "I can be persuasive, even if I do say so myself. Trina finally confessed that she was responsible for the stink bomb. It was designed to break open when it got jostled." He threw up his hands. "You know the rest of the story."

Clay waited to see how far Maizie's parents would take this tell-all session. Even though he was relieved that the stink bomb wasn't Maizie's handiwork, the fact of the matter was that Maizie didn't trust him. And reconciliation without faith wasn't possible.

Chapter Seventeen

The day after the beer basket fiasco, Maizie managed to stay busy at the Boudoir so the time passed quickly. Which was fortunate since she hadn't heard anything from Clay, not a single, solitary word.

Last night she'd been tempted to do bodily harm to Trina Carruthers. Damn that woman's hide! Thanks to Liza's clear head—and her assurance that they'd eventually get even—Maizie was able to set aside her thirst for revenge, at least for the moment.

The overriding issue now was how to make amends for the latest calamity. Clay had every right to be even angrier than he was before.

Later that afternoon, Maizie was unpacking a box of new inventory when Kenni strolled into the storeroom.

"I heard what happened last night. Bummer. Trina Carruthers is a piece of work."

Maizie continued to steam the wrinkles out of a skirt. "I think we should curse her with the fleas of a thousand camels. What do you think?"

"I say amen," Kenni agreed. "By the way, I talked to Aunt Eleanor today."

"What did she say?" Maizie couldn't hide her curiosity.

"Did you know your dad had a man-to-man talk with Clay last night? He told him it was all Trina's doing."

"What was Clay's reaction?" Maizie couldn't wait to hear what he'd had to say.

"Not much. Eleanor said he just kind of sat there."

That wasn't good. Clay almost always had an opinion, and didn't often hold back.

"Liza and I discussed the situation this morning. We think it's time to execute Operation: Brenda Lee." Kenni flashed a cheeky grin.

Maizie turned off the steamer. "How do you goofballs propose we do that?"

"I found us a Brenda." Kenni danced with excitement. "She sings at the Roadhouse Inn."

Her cousin was so proud of herself that Maizie almost hated to ask the next question, but she knew the Roadhouse Inn's reputation. The place was a dive.

"Who is she?"

"Her name's Roxy Ledbetter. She's one of Win's clients."

"Win, as in your husband, the criminal defense attorney?" Maizie asked.

"One and the same." Kenni had the gall to chuckle.

"Please tell me she's not a stripper or even worse—"

"Nothing like that. Roxy's a nice girl. She just has atrocious taste in men. Her skuzzy boyfriend implicated her in a case of grand theft auto and evading the cops. Win was able to get her out of it with nothing more than a fine, so she's beholden to him."

"Can she sing?"

"Of course." Kenni put her hands on her almost non-existent hips. "Do you think I'd recruit someone who couldn't sing? Are you nuts? And the really good news is that she specializes in the oldies so she knows the song."

Maizie wasn't quite as sold on the whole idea as her cohorts seemed to be.

Kenni continued, clearly not picking up on Maizie's lack of enthusiasm. "I talked to her today and told her we wanted a replay of the Romeo and Juliet balcony scene. Doesn't that sound awesome?"

"That's good, I guess." Maizie really wished she was more on board with this. "How much is this going to cost?"

"That's the best part. She's doing it for free because she likes Win."

"Free?"

"Yep, free as in no charge."

"Oh, okay. What time?"

"She has to be at the Inn by nine, so we agreed on eight o'clock tonight."

Maizie hugged her cousin. Even if the idea was goofy, she was touched by the effort. "You and Liza are the best. I don't know what I'd do without you."

"The feeling's mutual. You guys have saved my bacon more than once." Kenni grinned. "Do you think we can hide out in your mom's kitchen and watch?"

"I can guarantee Mama's gonna have a front row seat and I'm positive she'd loved the company." Maizie pulled her cordless out from under a pile of jeans and punched in her sister's number. "I'll give Liza a buzz and see if she can join us."

With luck this wouldn't turn into another calamity.

TYPICAL OF MAMA, SHE'D laid out a cocktail party spread appropriate for royalty—chilled wine, gourmet hors d'oeuvres and Godiva chocolate.

"Do you guys really think this will work?" Maizie asked for the millionth time. Although she thought it had a miniscule chance of succeeding, she wouldn't bet money on it.

Liza shrugged but didn't say a word. Kenni wasn't as restrained. "You two are as stubborn as a couple of mules. It's way past time for this to be over. So anything we do is better than sitting here twiddling our thumbs." Kenni slapped her hands together as if it was *a fait accompli.*

"Gee, thanks." Maizie knew she was stubborn but she didn't appreciate other people pointing it out. "Since when are you a philosopher?"

"I'm right and you know it," Kenni retorted. "Humor is the solution to this standoff."

When that girl was right, she was right. "Laughter has held our marriage together for years, so why go against a good thing?"

Chapter Eighteen

In the history of bad days, this one had been the worst. Clay and Harvey were heading back to their respective cars following a particularly harrowing meeting with their nemesis—the Department of Transportation planner.

When he and Harvey had bid on the engineering contract for a state highway interchange, they'd realized it would stretch their capabilities. But it had been too great an opportunity to pass up. Now halfway through the process the partners realized they'd made a gargantuan mistake.

There was one snafu after another. Clay should have recognized they were on shaky ground when he discovered they'd drawn the project manager from hell. In private, they called him a "banana"—an acronym for Build Absolutely Nothing Anywhere Near Anything. It was ironic considering his job was to facilitate the construction of highway projects.

His stringent demands were impossible to meet. Add to that an ill-timed spate of weather—an ice storm, torrential rains and a tornado—numerous delays in acquiring building materials, and it was impossible for the contractor to make the deadlines. And when the state started imposing penalties for noncompliance, it became painfully apparent that they were all going to be sucked into financial quicksand.

Harvey hit his remote locks. "What do you think will happen?"

Clay shook his head. Coming up with a solution would take a miracle.

"As long as we have that project manager, we're at an impasse. The fact is he doesn't want the interchange built and he plans to put up roadblocks at every turn."

"That's exactly what I thought." Harvey opened his car door. "How long do you think we have before we go under?"

"Six months or so." Clay unlocked his truck. "If we're lucky." Normally he was an optimist, but the way this situation was circling the drain, he wasn't holding out much hope.

"Let's meet tomorrow to see if we can come up with a way out of this mess."

"Sure, I'll be at the office around eight." Clay wasn't confident the situation was retrievable, but he was willing to try almost anything.

"I'd better get home. Sarah probably has dinner ready. I'll be in trouble if I'm not there to eat it."

Clay felt a stab of envy. His partner had a wife at home. What did he have to look forward to, other than bumming a meal off his in-laws? Eleanor hadn't said she was tired of feeding him, but he couldn't live off their charity forever.

With that depressing thought in mind, Clay stopped by the local drive-through to fill up on an artery-clogging meal of hamburger and fries. If he kept this up much longer his nickname was going to be Tubby.

Clay briefly considered driving through his neighborhood to catch a glimpse of Maizie. He loved her beyond reason. Nevertheless, he couldn't get past the fact that she'd tossed him out. Even worse, she'd kicked him when he was down. What had happened to their "till death" pledge?

Clay trudged up the stairs to the Westerfields' apartment knowing a cold beer and an empty bed was all that awaited him. A married man shouldn't be living like this. But what could he do to change it? Pride was terribly destructive. In this case Clay wasn't sure whether it was pride or hurt feelings that kept him from accepting Maizie's overtures.

He was pondering that situation, and flipping through the channels looking for something mindless to watch, when he heard a noise outside. Clay hit the Mute button. There was that sound again. It sounded like a cross between an out-of-tune banjo and a cat fight.

When Clay went out on the porch, he almost busted a gut laughing. What he'd thought was an amorous Tom cat was actually a woman in full cowgirl regalia belting out a song, accompanied by a karaoke boom box.

It took him a couple of seconds to realize she was singing Brenda Lee's "I'm Sorry." She was well into the second chorus of "so sorry, please accept my apology" before Clay managed to control his hilarity.

When he did, he leaned over the banister and bellowed, "Maizie Walker, get yourself out here. I want to talk to you."

"OH, MAN. I AM SO BUSTED." Hiding behind Mama's kitchen curtains, Maizie looked to her co-conspirators for moral support. Should she show her face?

"Go speak to him." Liza pushed her twin out the door, not giving her a chance to protest.

Maizie was about to make a U-turn when she heard the distinctive click of the dead bolt. Her sister had locked her out. With relatives like that, who needed enemies?

"What do you want?" She had to yell to be heard over the music. Good Lord, the entire neighborhood was being serenaded.

"What?" Clay put a hand to his ear, pantomiming that he couldn't hear her.

"What do— Oh, shoot." Maizie stomped over to "Brenda" and snapped off the boom box. "Thanks a million, Roxy. That was great." Sometimes a white lie was better than the truth. "Win has said such nice things about you."

The singer broke into a huge grin. "Mr. Whittaker is the greatest. He got me out of a mess of trouble, so I was glad to help."

Throughout this exchange Maizie could feel Clay staring at her. Too bad, manners came before settling a score, or fixing a fight, or whatever.

"Would you like help loading your equipment?"

"No, thanks, Ms. Walker. I keep my trusty karaoke machine in my car, so I'm used to lugging it around. No telling when someone might want you to break into song."

Maizie could honestly say that no one had ever asked her to sing.

Roxy stowed her microphone in her trunk and

waved to Clay. "Hope you liked that, Mr. Walker. Have a great evening, now ya hear."

She gave Maizie a wink before climbing into her car and pulling away.

Ooh-kay. Maizie felt like a minnow in a shark pool, what with Clay stomping down the stairs and all. Why was *he* frowning? Didn't he appreciate the song?

"Mary Stuart, what is this all about?" He waved a hand vaguely in the direction of Roxy's retreat.

"Uh." Maizie didn't know exactly what to say. She was hesitant to admit she was too chicken to talk to her own husband and had hired someone to do it for her. "I thought you might like some music?" She phrased her answer in the form of a question.

Clay gave her a long look before turning on his heel and walking back upstairs.

CLAY GRABBED ANOTHER BEER before plunking in front of the TV, finally letting out the chuckles he'd so carefully hidden from Maizie. How about that? Maizie had hired a Brenda Lee wannabe. He couldn't wait to see what she'd come up with next.

They'd both said a ton of things they didn't mean, but Clay was fairly confident they'd eventually reconcile. If Maizie was willing to make this big a fool of herself, she must still love him. Now it was time for him to show her he loved her, too.

Chapter Nineteen

Liza drove Maizie home following the ear-splitting serenade. "What did Clay say to you?"

"He asked what I thought I was doing."

Liza shot her a glance. "Is that all?"

"I couldn't tell for sure, but I think he was chuckling when he went upstairs." Maizie was searching for something positive. "That's good, isn't it?"

"It's wonderful."

"I hope so. What do you suggest I do next?"

Liza squinted the way she always did when she concentrated. "Let's wait a couple of days and then hit him again. We need something dramatic, something that'll knock his socks off."

"Do you have anything specific in mind?" Maizie wasn't convinced theatrics were the key, and that was unusual, given her proclivity for being over the top.

Liza pulled into Maizie's driveway and cut the engine. "Let me think about it." She leaned over the console and patted her sister's knee. "Don't worry, Clay will come around, you wait and see."

Maizie tried to stay optimistic. Things were looking up—sort of. "Sure. I'll call you tomorrow."

"Good. I have meetings all morning but I'll be in the office in the afternoon." Liza looked in the rearview mirror and chewed her lip.

"Do you know who owns that car, the silver one parked down there?" She nodded toward the vehicle in question.

Maizie turned to see what Liza was talking about. "No. Why?"

"I've seen it in various places on your street and that's kind of weird. Most people park in front of their house if they don't have space in their driveway."

"Have you noticed anyone sitting in it?" Could it be a police stakeout? She couldn't think of anyone suspicious in her neighborhood, but these days you just never knew.

"The windows are tinted so you can't see squat."

Maize stuck her head out the window trying to get a better view. "What do you think that's all about?"

"Beats me. It's probably nothing." Liza flipped the ignition and turned on her lights. "I'll wait until you're in the house."

"Thanks." Maizie unfolded her long legs from Liza's sports car. Normally she loved being tall, but there were certain limitations.

Maizie waved to her sister as she unlocked her front door, then watched Liza's car go around the corner before she took a good look at the car in question. It was unobtrusive and boring enough to be an undercover cop car—silver, tinted windows—nothing fancy or memorable. Or maybe someone in the neighborhood was having a fling and wanted to keep it quiet. Stranger things had happened.

Maizie wandered inside wondering what to do until it was time for bed. Being single was the pits. She could watch television—no, her tolerance for reality shows was waning. She could take a bubble bath—hmm, that had possibilities. She could snack—whoa, stop right there. Her hips could *not* take another Snickers binge.

Her favorite time of the day used to be when she and Clay would sit on the porch swing and talk. Now she was reduced to talking to herself. And to be perfectly blunt, her own conversation wasn't all that scintillating.

Chocolate. She needed some chocolate, and pretty darned quick. Maizie could almost hear the Häagen-Dazs mint chocolate-chip ice cream calling her name— to heck with her hips. She'd worry about it tomorrow.

Maizie rummaged through the freezer until she found a pint that wasn't crystallized. This was her lucky day. That thought lasted until the phone rang.

"Hey, Maizie, this is Carol Templeton, your neighbor." Carol had lived next door for almost fifteen years and she introduced herself every time she called. Did she really think Maizie would forget her?

"Hi, Carol, what's up?" She slipped a spoonful of ice cream into her mouth delighting in the texture and taste.

"Tim and I were wondering if you have a guest."

"No, why?" Carol was Laverne Hightower's protégé. *Please God say she hadn't noticed Clay's absence.* The chances of that were slim—the woman had eagle eyes and the nose of a bloodhound.

"Lately we've noticed a strange car driving up and down the street. It was parked near the Thompsons and now it's sitting in front of your house," she answered before yelling at the dog to get off the sofa.

"In front of *my* house?" Maizie asked. "*That's* creepy."

"That's what we thought. It's some sort of silver subcompact. Have you seen it?"

"Liza mentioned it tonight." Maizie's brain was racing a mile a minute.

Their neighborhood was usually peaceful—the only time they'd had trouble was when the Barker twins went wild with a roll of toilet paper.

"Don't go out there!" For a second Maizie was confused, then she realized Carol was talking to her husband.

"Gotta go." Her neighbor disconnected without bothering with the niceties.

Curiosity and Maizie had been good friends a long time, so of course she went out to see what was happening. She wasn't being nosy, no way; she was simply doing her neighborly duty.

Tim was stalking across her lawn toward the vehicle and Carol was right behind him. Maizie got ready to duck—just in case someone decided to pull a gun.

Fortunately it didn't get that far. The driver of the car saw Tim coming and threw it in Reverse so fast he hit the fire hydrant, knocking it over. The pulsating geyser sprayed water all over the neighborhood.

The perp popped the car into Drive, hit the gas and sped away before anyone could jot down a license number. The way he skidded and screeched out of the neighborhood would have made Smokey and the Bandit proud.

"What do you think that was all about?" Maizie had to yell to be heard over the sound of gushing water.

"I don't know," Tim answered. "But I think it's time for a meeting of our neighborhood watch. Hey, guys." He whistled to get the attention of the small band of people who had emerged from their houses to investigate the commotion. "Let's meet at our house tomorrow around seven to discuss this. We'll get someone from the sheriff's office to join us. Maizie, would you call your brother-in-law?"

"Certainly." Personally she thought a meeting was overkill, but right now she'd do anything to keep the peace. The whole incident was probably nothing more than a horny high school kid trying to get a girl's attention.

Ah, the nostalgia. Way back when, Maizie was in junior high, she'd had an "admirer" who'd lingered on her street for hours. Every time she went outside he'd scurry over to ask her for a date. That was before Daddy threatened him within an inch of his life.

Those were the days—thin thighs and a bevy of beaus.

Chapter Twenty

The flow of customers at the Boudoir didn't let up until late the following afternoon. If they'd been buyers that would have been great, but Maizie suspected they were browsers and curiosity hounds. A few were interested in the car hitting the hydrant, but since there were so few specifics about that, Maizie knew most were being drawn in by something even more spectacular.

It wasn't until nearly closing time that her suspicion was confirmed. *Everyone* in town had heard about Brenda Lee.

"You know about the serenade, don't you, PJ?" Maizie didn't really want to hear the answer, but she couldn't help herself.

Her friend responded with a giggle. Traitor.

"I'm so embarrassed." Maizie slapped her hands on the top of her head. "The people who came in today wanted to gawk, didn't they?"

"Probably." If possible, PJ's grin got even wider. "But think about it. You girls are becoming a legend. People can't wait to see what you'll do next. I think it's way cool."

"You do?" Maizie couldn't imagine why making a

fool of one's self would be considered cool, but different strokes and all that rot.

Before PJ could answer, the bell on the door tinkled announcing another customer—hopefully a paying one this time.

No such luck. The queen of all window shoppers would be better than the person who strolled in.

"Oh, boy. Color me gone," PJ muttered, quickly retreating to the back room

Maizie was left to face Cora Lee Tillington, society editor for the *Magnolia Bluffs Gazette*. Cora was the same generation as Mama and Daddy and she knew everyone in town—except maybe the folks out in the trailer park, but even that wasn't a sure bet.

What was it they said about soothing the savage breast? Speak with a comforting voice and show no fear. "Hey there, Cora Lee," Maizie said, displaying her best beauty pageant smile. "What can I do for you?"

"Mary Stuart, honey, it's more what I can do for you." Cora Lee Tillington had obviously seen too many movies. With her outdated business suit and a pencil stuck in her graying bun, she looked like a female Social Security version of Bob Woodward.

"I give. What can you do for me?" Maizie couldn't resist.

"The entire town is buzzing about what you girls are up to. So what's next?"

"I'm sorry. I don't have any idea what you mean." This situation definitely called for playing the blond bimbo card.

"Please. I've known you since you were in diapers. You can't BS an old BS'er."

Playing dumb hadn't worked. Maybe distraction would. "Can I perhaps interest you in one of our wonderful bras?" Maizie pulled a lacy push-up off the rack. "Or a new sundress." She headed straight for a strapless polished-cotton number more suitable for a teenager than one of Mama's contemporaries.

Cora Lee retrieved a battered notebook from her voluminous purse. "I want the straight skinny and no more messin' around. My readers are dying to know what's coming up next. I hear you're going to hire a brass band. Is that right?" She had her pencil poised to jot down Maizie's answer.

A brass band—now that was an interesting idea.

Cora Lee interrupted Maizie's ruminations. "If you can draw this thing out for a month, I'll make it a regular column." The *Gazette* came out twice a week and the dingbat wanted Maizie to come up with a show for each issue?

"That isn't going to happen. Believe me."

Cora Lee's glasses slipped further down her nose. "Oh, well, it was merely a thought. At least give me an exclusive on your next shenanigan."

It was obvious that Cora wasn't giving up—and Maizie had had enough for one day—so she decided to throw the reporter a bone.

"I don't have a specific date, but yes, a brass band is in the works."

Cora's eyebrows shot straight into her hairline.

Great. Maizie's big mouth was getting her in trouble again. Tuba players didn't exactly advertise in the phone book, so where was she going to find someone to play John Phillip Sousa? Aha! The high school band director's wife was a regular customer, so maybe—

"This is marvelous, simply marvelous." Cora scribbled in her notebook. "You be sure to let me know when it's going to happen, ya hear? The paper comes out on Wednesday and Saturday, so if you'll call me the day before, I'm sure I can drum up an audience." Cora poked the pencil back in her bun.

An audience? That was almost as good as doing a marriage proposal on national TV—saying no was virtually impossible.

Cora Lee was on her way out the door when she lobbed a parting shot. "I hear there's a family betting pool."

A betting pool? Did she really say there was a betting pool? The nerve of it all.

"PJ, you can come out now." Maizie used her best syrupy-sweet voice to lure the poor insect into her spider's web.

Sure enough, it worked. PJ peeked around the corner. "Is she gone?"

"She certainly is." Maizie could do innocent with the best of them. "Come on out. Really now, would I lie?"

PJ reluctantly made her way to the counter. "Ms. Tillington gives me the willies."

Maizie couldn't agree more. Cora Tillington was definitely nervous-making. "She told me something interesting."

Maizie went to the front door and turned over the Closed sign.

PJ took that as a signal to tally up the day's receipts. "Really? What?"

"Cora Lee said there's a family betting pool—I assume on how soon Clay and I will get together." Maizie leaned over the counter to get nose-to-nose with her employee. "What do you know about that?"

At first PJ looked shocked, but then her expression changed to guilt. "Why would I know anything?"

Maizie stepped back. More than likely, PJ was the family bookie.

"Because you're privy to everything that goes on around here?" Maizie knew full well that PJ was up to her cute little kneecaps in it.

"Hey, it wasn't my idea." The assistant manager put her hands up in the air. "Your mom's the ringleader."

"Mama? My mother organized a betting pool?"

"Yep. Her money's on twenty-eight days. I think she said something about you guys being mulish. Your aunt Anna Belle is much more optimistic. She went for a week."

Good going, Auntie Anna Belle. At least Kenni's mother had faith.

"What about my sister?" Maizie couldn't wait to hear Liza's take.

"She's got ten days. She thinks that after a couple more 'visitations'—" PJ emphasized the word with finger quotes, "—he'll scurry over to the bright side."

"Liza's always been an optimist. What about you? I'm sure you plunked down your ante."

PJ had the chutzpah to giggle. "My guess is even longer than your mom's. I work for you, remember?"

Chapter Twenty-One

It had been almost a week since the Brenda Lee incident and the fact that he hadn't seen or heard from Maizie was making Clay nervous. In this case, no news wasn't necessarily good news.

But enough worrying about his errant wife—work was calling. Boy, was it ever.

Clay was engrossed in deciphering a spreadsheet when Harvey appeared in his office doorway. "What's up, partner?" Clay took his reading glasses off and laid them on his desk.

"Have you seen the paper this morning?" Harvey whipped a copy of the *Magnolia Bluffs Gazette* out from behind his back.

"No, why? Do they have a special on pot roasts at the Piggly Wiggly?" Clay thought he'd come up with a decent comeback, until he took a good look at his friend's grin.

Clay rounded the desk and snatched the newspaper out of Harvey's hand.

"Here's a clue. Try Cora Lee's page." Uh-oh. His partner was smirking.

"Oh, God," he moaned. "Please tell me Maizie hasn't completely lost her mind."

Harvey pointedly said nothing before he exited.

An Invitation To A Two-Fer—A Brass Quartet Recital And Chapter Three Of The War Of The Walkers. *That* was the headline of the society section.

"Harvey!" Clay was halfway down the hall before he noticed his staff. The women were giggling and the men were giving him their best "you poor sucker" looks.

"Harvey!" He stormed into his partner's office waving the paper. "Did you know this was coming?"

Harvey's eloquent shrug said it all.

Was the entire town conspiring against him? No sooner had that thought occurred to Clay than he heard music. It wasn't ordinary music—au contraire—he distinctly heard a tuba.

"*What* is that?"

"You'd better go check it out," Harvey wheezed through his laughter. "We have a few visitors in the lobby."

Clay shot him a rude hand gesture as he hurried out to the lobby. A few people! Hell, there were people all over the reception area and spilling out the front door. Didn't they have anything better to do than watch his humiliation?

In the middle of the crowd was the local high school's marching band—complete with uniforms and feathered hats. Great, now a bunch of teenagers were involved in what Cora Lee had dubbed the War of the Walkers. Oh, the joys of living in a small town.

The tuba player was the first to spot him. "Hey, Mr. Walker. We came to play for you." He turned to his fellow musicians. "Here we go. A one, a two and a three." When he nodded, the music almost blasted Clay out of the room.

Clay wasn't too well-versed in brass band music, but the selection sounded vaguely familiar. "What was the name of that song?" he asked when the band quit playing.

The trumpet player was the first to speak up. "It was Sousa's version of the 'Wedding March.' Way buck, huh?"

"Very buck," Clay agreed, not having a clue what that meant. And clever. How in the world had Maizie pulled this off?

"Here's a message." The trombone player pulled an envelope from his pocket. "It's from your wife."

Clay couldn't wait to see what she'd written so he opened the envelope right there in the lobby. It was an apology done Maizie style that made him laugh. That girl had a way about her. Sometimes he couldn't decide whether to kiss her or throttle her, and that's what made their marriage so good. So why was he holding out? Could they regain the trust they once had? Maizie seemed to think so. Clay wasn't quite so sure.

Okay, Maizie and her buddies had had their last shot at theatrical comedy. The courting was going to begin in earnest. And this time he planned to do it right. No more burgers and drive-in movies. They'd start all over and see if they could get through this rough patch.

MAIZIE AND LIZA HAD THEIR noses pressed against the tearoom window across the street from Clay's office. Although it wasn't exactly a ringside seat, they could see the crowd, and what a crowd it was. With the right incentive, Cora Lee could recruit a cast of thousands.

"Do you see him?" Maizie asked. Her heart was beating a mile a minute wondering how Clay would react to the ruckus.

"Over there!" Liza pointed to the side door of the engineering firm. She was literally bouncing in her chair.

"Where?" Maizie scanned the area several times before she spotted him. He was tall, blond and handsome as all get-out—and he was holding a handmade sign that read, "Maizie Walker you're a naughty girl. Give me a call."

Maizie didn't know whether he could see her through the window, but a couple of minutes later Clay waved, did a thumbs-up and walked back into the office. Darn him—he thought he was in charge here. He wasn't, was he?

Maizie was so busy thinking about her husband's request that she missed the fact someone had come up behind her and Liza.

"Hello, ladies. May I join you?" It was Trip Fitzgerald, looking as buff as ever.

"Yeah, okay," Liza answered, scooting over to make room for the newcomer.

"Hi, Trip. I haven't seen you in a while. What have you been doing?" Although Maizie wasn't at all interested in him—other than as a friend—that didn't mean she couldn't be polite.

"A little of this, a little of that. Mostly working. Are you coming back to the club soon?" Trip grabbed a scone from the plate in the center of the table.

"Probably not, I'm swamped at the boutique," Maizie said with a shrug. "I thought I could make the time, but it hasn't worked out."

"I can do a private lesson whenever you want. You name it and I'm yours." He took a bite of the purloined scone.

"That's so sweet. I'll let you know."

"Okay." He turned to look out the window. "I presume you ladies are responsible for the excitement across the street?"

"That's right." Liza said.

"Cora's column called this the War of the Walkers. Is that correct?"

"I wouldn't believe everything that's in the paper." It was too embarrassing to talk about this with the man who was indirectly responsible for the argument with Clay, so Maizie changed the subject. "Would you like a cup of tea to go along with your pastry?"

"Sure, do you have an extra mug?"

Maizie motioned to the waitress, who brought one over.

The three of them sat quietly for a few moments. Trip took a sip of his tea before he picked up Maizie's hand. "I'm serious about the private lessons. Let me know if you change your mind. I'm available." He put down his cup and strolled off, ignoring the admiring looks he was getting from various females.

Liza waited until he was out the door before she said something. "Does he have a crush on you?"

Maizie laughed thinking of all the times Trip had seen her soaked in sweat. Was she kidding? "Don't be silly. We're really good friends. He has size zeros fawning all over him, so there's no way he'd be interested in a middle-aged married woman."

Chapter Twenty-Two

"Can you believe Maizie was able to talk a brass quartet into playing for you?" Harvey buttered a piece of corn-bread and stuffed it into his mouth. It was fried chicken night at the DeLite Diner.

Clay had been chuckling ever since the last tuba note. "I'm going to marry that girl. That is, if we can ever get back on the right path."

Harvey gave him a strange look. "Please don't tell me you guys aren't married. That would shatter all my illusions of matrimony." Harvey had been married twice and was intent on making sure the third time stuck.

"What I meant is that I plan to court her. And after I win her over I'll broach the subject of renewing our vows. We were so young when we started dating that all I could afford was an occasional Coke, and that wasn't too often. This time around I'm going to pull out all the stops."

"That sounds like a plan to me." Harvey quickly forgot his manners when the waitress delivered their food. "Do you know anything about romance?" he asked around a mouthful of mashed potatoes.

That was a good question. Clay wondered whether there was a *Romance for Dummies* book.

"Not much," he admitted. "I suppose the first thing I should do is make a reservation at a classy restaurant."

"With tablecloths," Harvey added.

"Tablecloths are definitely a plus, and it should have some expensive wines. We'll make small talk and then I'll hold her hand and look into her eyes. We'll eat, but I won't talk with my mouth full. I'll surrender my credit card and that should do the trick. Is that about it?"

"Sounds good to me, but what do I know? I popped the question to wife number two at the bowling alley."

"And how long did that one last?" Clay tempered his comment with a grin.

"I see what you mean," Harv admitted sheepishly.

IT HAD BEEN A *HIDEOUSLY* long day. Both Liza and Mama were harassing Maizie to call Clay. But that wasn't going to happen. It was his turn to take action. She'd already provided a stink bomb, an ersatz Brenda Lee and a brass band. What more did he want?

Dinner was a reheated pot pie and a wilted salad. Clay was probably enjoying fried chicken and peach cobbler—courtesy of either her mother or the DeLite Diner. It wasn't fair, but Maizie couldn't blame anyone but herself.

Pity parties were such a drag. So with a glass of wine in hand, she was getting ready to slip into a bubble bath when the phone rang. Hoping it was Clay and praying it wasn't Mama, Maizie grabbed the cordless and chirped a greeting.

"Mo-o-om," Her daughter was the only person Maizie knew who could turn that one-syllable word into about three. "What's going on at home? I went online to read the *Gazette,* just to check out what was happening and there it was in black and white. The War of the Walkers. What do you guys think you're doing?"

Hannah was in a snit. Hadn't Maizie's day sucked enough already?

"Honey, everything's fine. Your dad and I are having a little disagreement and the paper got involved. You know how it is around here. Everyone knows everyone else's business."

"Are you getting divorced?"

"No way." Please God let her be telling the truth. "It's not that big a deal. I promise."

"Are you sure?"

"Honestly."

"I want to talk to Daddy."

What could Maizie say? "Well, uh, your dad is staying at Grammy's house."

There was a long pause before Hannah wailed. "He's not living with you?"

"No," Maizie admitted.

"That does it! I'm coming home."

"Please don't. You have to go to class. We're fine, honestly we are." Hannah was a bigger drama queen than Maizie and they truly didn't need any more hysteria. "Call your daddy. He'll tell you the same thing."

"Okay, but if I get any bad vibes I'm coming home."

Maizie couldn't argue with that. And she wasn't worried. Even when Hannah was a baby Clay could calm her.

"I love you, sweetie. Don't worry about us." Maizie was doing enough of that on her own. "We're fine."

"I love you, too, Mama." Hannah didn't call her mama unless she was really upset.

"Get a good night's sleep."

"Okay. But I'm serious—if I hear anything else I'll be home like a shot."

"That's fair enough." If Cora Tillington dared mentioned the name Walker in that rag again, Maizie would sue her sweet buns.

After a few more minutes of reassuring her daughter, Maizie placed the cordless on the bathroom vanity in anticipation of hopping in the tub. That fantasy evaporated when she heard a loud crash downstairs. It didn't sound like breaking glass. Maybe one of the neighbors' cats had knocked something off the porch. She shook her head, determined not to worry.

Maizie had one toe in the suds before she decided to check, just in case. She grabbed her bathrobe and the phone before tiptoeing downstairs. Sneaky was her middle name.

Using every ounce of stealth she could muster, Maizie went out the back door and quietly made her way toward the front yard. Damn, it was dark!

Taking one step at a time she crept along the side of the house. Wow, she was good at this covert ops stuff. That thought pinged through her brain right before she stubbed her toe, sending pain shooting straight to the top of her head. Don't cuss, don't scream and for God's sake, don't even whimper.

Maizie was almost to the edge of the house when she heard muttering. Nope, that wasn't a cat. Think—what were her options? Take the creep out with a brilliant kung-fu maneuver? Call 911? That was the winner.

As Maizie punched in the numbers she carefully peeked around the corner. She must have made a noise because the man peering in her front window turned, looked around wildly and then ran full-tilt toward the end of the porch.

Maizie should have been relieved he was hauling ass—too bad he was on a collision course with the spot where she was hunkered down. She had no more than a second to brace herself before the intruder leaped over the porch rail, crashed through an azalea and landed smack-dab on top of her.

The breath whooshed out of her lungs and she immediately saw a whole galaxy of stars. Scream! Oh, yeah. She'd do that as soon as she could breathe.

Even in her state of sheer terror Maizie noticed a few things about her attacker: he wasn't waving a knife, he was dressed all in black including a ski mask, and he appeared to be almost as discombobulated as she was. How about that, an incompetent burglar.

"Nine-one-one, what is your emergency?" The tinny voice coming from the phone Maizie still clutched kept repeating the question.

When the intruder heard that, he jumped up and ran off. Not fond of cops, huh?

"Uh." Maizie finally managed to at least groan.

"Ma'am, are you all right?" Too bad she still couldn't quite speak. "Ma'am? I'm sending a unit to your home. Stay on the line until they get there."

"Uh-huh." That was the extent of Maizie's conversational skills.

Five minutes later two police cars arrived, lights blazing and sirens wailing. That was when Maizie realized she was wearing nothing but a threadbare chenille bathrobe. Holy catfish! Talk about adding insult to injury.

"Maizie, what happened? Are you all right?" She should've guessed her brother-in-law would be one of the respondents. "I heard your address on the scanner and I came right over."

"I'm okay, I think, although I do need to get dressed."

Maizie cinched the belt of the robe. "I thought I had an intruder so I came out to see what was going on. I was at the end of the porch when he jumped off and landed on me." She paused for a second, afraid she might pass out. "He scared me silly and knocked the breath out of me, but I'm okay."

"These nice folks are here to check you out." Zack turned to the two young paramedics. "This is my sister-in-law, take good care of her."

"Yes, sir." The EMT was a dead ringer for Brad Pitt. Wasn't that just her darned luck.

"You probably won't like this but I'm calling Liza," Zack said as he punched in some numbers on his cell. "She'll have my hide if I don't."

Then Liza would call Kenni and so on. From there it would only be a matter of minutes before the entire family would come rushing to the rescue—and the only thing saving her from being bare-ass naked was her ratty bathrobe.

It was the perfect end to a perfect day.

Chapter Twenty-Three

Liza was the first family member to arrive, followed by Mama and Daddy, then Kenni and Win, and later ex-sheriff Dave and Aunt Eugenie showed up. So where was Clay? Maizie's question was answered when his truck rounded the corner on two wheels and screeched to a stop.

"Damn it!" Clay barreled through the front door and grabbed her by the shoulders. He didn't bother with any niceties. "Why didn't you call me?"

That did it! Maizie planted her hands on her hips, ready to tear a strip off his hide. "Do you really care?" Sarcasm dripped from her every word.

Clay glared but he didn't say anything else. She couldn't tell whether he was about to let her have it or go for the glacial treatment. Normally they preferred a rip-roaring row and then have spectacular make-up sex. But this was beyond anything they'd had to face before.

Clay let go of her shoulders and went over to talk to Zack who nodded and turned to the crowd.

"Everyone, listen up. The excitement's over. Let's

all head to our cars and leave Maizie and Clay to sort this one out."

Zack's announcement earned him a dirty look from his wife, but that didn't stop him. "Come on, chop, chop. Let's move this circus on down the road."

Maizie giggled. That man didn't have a chance in hell of sleeping in Liza's bed tonight. If he was lucky the dogs would let him bunk in with them.

Liza glared at her husband one more time. She wasn't used to being separated from her sister—especially in a time of trouble. She put her arms around Maizie. "I'll call you in the morning. If you need anything tonight, give me a buzz. I don't care how late."

After the police had finished their somewhat limited investigation and the crowd had dispersed Clay made himself at home, retrieving a beer from the refrigerator and a bag of chips from the pantry.

Maizie picked up his brew and took a sip. "Aren't you leaving?" She tried to sound nonchalant.

"Nope, I'm tired of your mother's accommodations. I'm moving into Hannah's room. Do you have a problem with that?"

"No, I suppose not." Hallelujah! She wasn't going to have to stay awake all night worrying about being murdered in her bed.

That was the only piece of good news. She wasn't worried, but Clay's proposed arrangements were a guaranteed recipe for insomnia. Hours later—after she'd punched her pillow, rolled over at least four hundred times and checked the clock so often the glowing numbers were burned into her eyes—Maizie conceded there was something far worse than fending off a homicidal maniac. That was sleeping down the hall from a husband she desperately wanted to ravage, or at the very least have her way with.

Men were such pigs. He was probably sound asleep while she was agonizing over her desire to pay him a naughty visit. She was dying to get back to her normal, boring life. But considering everything that had gone down, could they really make things right?

It was shortly before dawn before Maizie finally drifted off to sleep. Her last coherent thought was that she was going to feel like a pile of dog doo when the alarm buzzed.

Boy, did she call that one right. A tequila bender would have been better. At least she would have had the fun of getting drunk. Someone was pounding a bongo in her head, her stomach was queasy and her hair looked like Medusa with a perm. It wasn't a great start to the morning.

Maizie stumbled down the stairs in search of a cup of coffee. But instead of coffee she discovered a full breakfast—bacon, eggs, grits and toast. It was Nirvana wrapped in cholesterol.

"Hey, Sunshine, I was about to come up and wake you. Don't you have to go to work?"

"Uh-huh." Maizie was too focused on procuring a caffeine fix to be more eloquent than that.

"Sorry," she said after savoring her first sip. "You cooked me breakfast. That was so sweet." Actually, it made her want to cry.

Clay piled her plate high with food. "Sit down and eat."

That was an order she gladly obeyed. Food was exactly what she needed.

"This is delicious." The scrambled eggs were perfect, the bacon was crisp, the grits were buttery and the coffee was strong—it was a chubby girl's version of heaven.

"Maizie, we need to talk." Clay toyed with his mug.

A man who wanted to talk? Gabriel must be tooting his horn. Either that or the four horsemen were about to ride through the kitchen.

"I'm going to move back in. Don't freak. I'll bunk in Hannah's room." He didn't give her time to argue, not that she wanted to. "I don't think it's safe for you to be here by yourself."

"Why?"

Clay shrugged. "Zack told me about the fire hydrant incident." He frowned. "By the way, why didn't *you* tell me about that?"

"I didn't think you'd be interested." The truth was she afraid he wouldn't care.

"I wouldn't be interested!" he shouted. "Are you out of your freakin' mind?"

That was a valid question. She had been acting a little nutty lately, but Maizie knew a good thing when she saw it, and having her husband at home was fantastic— even if he wasn't ready to come back to their bed. The best part was that Clay thought it was all his idea.

Chapter Twenty-Four

Clay felt as fuzzy-brained as his wife. How could he sleep down the hall from Maizie night after night, and still be able to function?

If today was any indication, it wasn't going to be easy. He'd arrived late to the office and had just pulled up a file on the computer when a familiar voice called a halt to anything work related.

"Hi, Daddy."

He looked up from his monitor to find his daughter standing in his office doorway.

"Hey, Sweetie!" Although it was a pleasant surprise, Hannah was the very last person Clay expected, or wanted, to see. Especially the way things were going at home. He went around the desk to give his daughter a hug.

"What are you doing here? Don't you have classes?" Clay didn't give her a chance to answer before he continued. "Grab us a couple of Cokes while I close out this program."

Hannah rummaged through the minifridge and came up with two soft drinks.

"Here you go." She placed both cans on the coffee table and then took a seat on the couch.

Clay glanced at his little girl who wasn't so little anymore. Even so, she was giving him the same "take no prisoners look" she'd perfected as a preschooler. And she still hadn't answered his question.

"Why are you here?" He joined her on the couch, not quite certain what to expect.

"I want to know what's going on with you and Mom." Hannah had never been one to mince words— a trait she shared with Maizie and Liza.

How could you explain the goat rope this escapade had become other than by admitting that two incredibly stubborn people were butting heads? "Don't worry about us. We're having a simple disagreement that has unfortunately gotten some attention in the local press." He shrugged as if to say, "What can you do?" "You know what it's like in Magnolia Bluffs."

"A disagreement? You call being a regular feature in the paper a *disagreement?*"

Clay had been a parent long enough to recognize the start of a crying binge.

"Hannah, honey. Honestly, it started off as a spat and somehow it escalated. I'm back at home now. There's nothing to worry about." He didn't tell her he was camped out in her bedroom, nor did he mention his "courting Maizie" project.

"Are you going by the boutique to see your mom?"

Hannah shook her head. "No, I don't think so. I talked to her last night."

She looked so much like the little girl he remembered that it was as though time had stood still.

"Promise me you have it covered." Her request was just short of a whine.

"Don't worry I'm on it." Clay could only hope he wasn't kidding himself.

MAIZIE COULDN'T CONCENTRATE on retail to save her life and PJ wasn't helping matters.

"I heard what happened last night. That is so scary!" PJ exclaimed wringing her hands. "Are you really okay?"

"Other than not getting any sleep and feeling like crap with a capital C, I'm fine. Honestly," Maizie assured her friend.

"Okay, if you're absolutely positive." PJ didn't bother to hide her lascivious grin. "I understand Clay spent the night."

"Lord in heaven, nothing's secret in this town!" Maizie exclaimed. "Tell me exactly what you heard, and don't leave anything out."

PJ smirked again. "Just that you were chasing a prowler and he attacked you. And you and Clay spent the night having wild monkey sex." She laughed at her own wit. "Fine, so I made up that last part."

"Typical. Only half of that's true. Why don't people get their stories straight?"

"So what is true? And to quote my boss, don't leave anything out."

Maizie plunked her butt on the fainting couch, knowing full well PJ wouldn't take no for an answer.

"Yes, I had a prowler. But no, he didn't attack me. He must've panicked when he heard me coming around from the backyard and that's when he leaped off the porch. Unfortunately he landed right on top of me. And believe me—in that situation, being on the bottom wasn't any fun."

Thank goodness her sense of humor had finally kicked in. "As for the monkey sex, I only wish. Clay spent the night in Hannah's room." Maizie made a tsking sound. "I'm not sure what any of it means."

"Darn. That wasn't nearly as juicy as I'd hoped."

"However." Maizie drew out the word for dramatic effect. "The reason I'm so tired is that I was up all night fantasizing about all sorts of prurient activities."

PJ fanned herself. "Whew."

Lunch came and went and Maizie still hadn't perked up. She was tired, she was cranky and she needed some exercise.

"PJ, can you do without me for a couple of hours this afternoon? I'd like to go take a tennis lesson. Maybe some fresh air and a workout will get me out of this funk."

"I didn't know you were still playing."

"I haven't in a while. I was trying to behave and keep my mind on business."

"You get out of here. We won't even miss you," PJ said with a grin.

"Thanks a million."

"MAIZIE! IT'S GREAT TO see you."

"Hi, Trip. I hope you don't mind me dropping in for a group lesson."

"Are you funnin' me? I'm delighted to have you back. In fact, I have some ladies who are looking for a fourth. Are you interested?"

"How desperate are they?"

Trip laughed but didn't contradict her. So that's how it was. Desperate was good.

"As long as they're not expecting Wimbledon quality I'm your gal." Wimbledon, ha! She wouldn't be allowed within a hundred miles of the stadium.

"They're nice. You know Paige Butler."

"Sure, I do."

"You'll have a good time with them. I promise."

Maizie certainly hoped he was right. Good times had been few and far between lately.

Chapter Twenty-Five

Exercise was exactly what Maizie needed. She tore up the court with killer volleys and awesome lobs. Her forehand was sizzling and her backhand was mean. Not really, but she was at least able to keep it inside the white lines. And to her way of thinking, that was amazing progress.

Maizie was feeling better by the time she got home and discovered three new additions—Clay's keys on the kitchen counter, his suitcase in the hall and a steaming-hot box of Giorgio's Pizza on the table. The suitcase and keys meant another sleepless night, but the pizza was another story. It was manna from heaven, food of the gods, damned near perfect.

"I thought we'd do take-out tonight." Clay had somehow managed to sneak into the kitchen while Maizie's attention had been diverted by the pepperoni-and-double-cheese pizza, dripping in calories and butter fat.

"Are you staying here tonight?" Maizie wasn't sure whether she wanted him to. Especially if he was going to insist on sleeping down the hall.

"Yep. That's why I brought my toothbrush. Like I

told you, I'm not leaving you here by yourself, not while there's a prowler on the loose." And not even when they caught the bastard and threw him in jail, but he wasn't about to tell his wife that.

Clay Walker was on a mission to salvage their marriage. Maizie had made the first move and now it was his turn.

He plucked his cell from his belt, punched in a few numbers and almost immediately the kitchen phone rang. Maizie gave him a funny look, but nevertheless she picked up the receiver and managed a perfunctory hello.

"This is Clay Walker. May I speak to Maizie?" With that bit of silliness he winked.

"Speaking."

"Miss Maizie, would you like to go out to dinner with me tomorrow night?" He leaned against the counter, never breaking eye contact.

"Uh." Well, look at that. She was speechless.

"I've made reservations at Antoine's in Atlanta. We'll have a romantic dinner and a good bottle of wine. What do you think?"

For a brief moment Maizie wondered whether they could afford it. Then her fiddle-dee-dee philosophy kicked in. Since Clay was being so sweet she'd worry about money later.

"I'd love to. What time?"

"I'll pick you up around six."

Why on earth would he pick her up if he was staying at the house?

THE QUESTION WAS ANSWERED the next evening. While Maizie was agonizing about what to wear, Clay had disappeared. Half her wardrobe had ended up either on the floor or on her bed before she finally settled on an outfit that was dressy enough without being too dressy, sexy enough without being overt and best of all, easy to remove—piece by tantalizing piece. But where was her husband? It was almost six now and he was nowhere to be found.

If this was some kind of sick joke she was gonna kill him. She'd barely finished that homicidal thought when the doorbell rang. Now what?

Maizie flung open the door expecting to see Liza or Mama, but no, it was Clay, all dressed up and looking as handsome as sin.

"What are you doing ringing the doorbell?"

The wink he gave her was a fascinating combination of conspiratorial fun and lascivious interest. "I'm picking up my date." He pulled a bouquet of wild flowers out from behind his back.

Maizie almost swooned. He'd never been one for romantic gestures before. "Okay, what are you up to? Did you do something that's gonna get you in trouble?"

Clay looked surprised, and then broke out laughing. "I'm courting you, you silly goose. Grab your purse and let's get rolling."

Five minutes later they were in Clay's pickup on their way to Atlanta. They'd been married over twenty years and Maizie couldn't think of anything to say. This felt like a first date, and that was incredibly uncomfortable.

"How about those Falcons?" If that was the best she could come up with, it was going to be a very long night. The Atlanta NFL team was tail-end Charlie in the

National Football Conference South division, so that discussion could only last about two minutes.

"I don't think they'll win on Sunday, do you?" she asked.

Clay answered with a shrug and that was the tone of the entire trip, at least until the truck started going thumpty, thumpty, thump.

He smacked the steering wheel as he pulled off the highway. "That's effin' fantastic. I think we have a flat tire."

"Do you have a spare?"

"Yeah." Clay jumped from the truck and ripped off his jacket. Then he leaned back into the cab. "This isn't what I'd planned for our first date."

No kidding!

By the time they made it to the restaurant, Clay's formerly white shirt was smeared with grease, sweat was running off his face and Maizie was exhausted from watching him work. Lord only knew what would happen during dinner.

Clay pulled into the parking lot and cut the engine. "Tell you what. Let's bag this idea and do something we'll both enjoy. I'm not sure they'll even let me in looking like this."

Although Maizie was delighted, she couldn't resist pulling his chain. "Oh, but I was looking forward to a fancy dinner and an extravagant bottle of wine."

Clay's face fell, but he recovered nicely. "Okay. Let's go." He pulled the keys from the ignition and opened his door.

Maizie put her hand on his knee. "I was just kidding. Let's do something fun. This little number will go anywhere." She held out her hands indicating the black designer dress she was wearing. "And you look like you've been Dumpster diving."

Clay laughed. "Are you impugning my hygiene?"

"No way. I'm sure you showered this week." In the summer Clay bathed a couple of times a day. It felt good to joke with him again.

"I'll tell you what. Let's go to either the Big Chicken or the Varsity," he suggested.

All roads in Atlanta led to the Big Chicken in northwest Atlanta. In 1963 an enterprising greasy spoon owner "hatched" the idea of building the world's largest postmodern cubist steel chicken to attract customers. Through thick and thin, the chicken had endured, even though it was now a KFC, complete with buckets of thighs and legs.

The Varsity had been an Atlanta landmark for over eighty years. Located near the Georgia Tech campus it was famous for hot dogs, onion rings, fried pies and frosted orange drinks. The college kids considered it junk food heaven.

"Let's do the Varsity." Maizie almost licked her lips in anticipation of a chili dog with onions and a peach fried pie. It wasn't traditional date food, but she did have a stash of mints in her purse.

"That sounds *really* good." Clay fired up the engine and pointed the truck toward the Varsity.

THEY TALKED, HELD HANDS and acted like kids in love. Maizie couldn't wait to get her husband home and out of that suit. So when Clay stopped in front of the house without bothering to pull into the drive, she was confused. Where did he think he was going?

Her motto had always been when in doubt, ask. "Aren't you staying here?"

He didn't answer. "Don't move a muscle. I'm coming around to open your door." He hadn't done that since they were teenagers and he was still trying to impress her.

Clay helped Maizie out of the truck and walked her to the front door. "I had a lot of fun tonight."

"I did, too. We need to do this more often." She leaned forward expecting a kiss—the wetter and hotter the better.

"I did, too. And believe me, I plan for us to have more date nights," Clay said, but instead of pulling her into his arms, he took her hand and shook it. Then the jerk turned and walked back down the sidewalk.

"Clayton Walker, where do you think you're going?" she hollered, not giving a flying fig what the neighbors thought.

He looked over his shoulder. His grin was a killer. "I plan to get in my truck and drive around the block. Then I'm going to sneak in the back door and hide out in Hannah's room, right after I have a long cold shower."

Maizie stomped down the stairs to confront her husband. "Why are you doing that?"

"Because I don't think we should kiss on our first date." And with that silly announcement, he kissed her on the end of her nose.

Maizie wanted to whack him upside the head. "So you're really not planning to come back to our bed?" She managed to lower her voice so at least not *all* the neighbors would hear their conversation.

"Not until we've dated awhile. I wouldn't want you to think I'm easy." His grin got even bigger, if that was possible. "I'll see you in the morning."

He strolled down the sidewalk, got in the truck and drove away.

Chapter Twenty-Six

"So how was your date?" Liza asked. It was their traditional Tuesday morning southern comfort breakfast at Daisy's Dining Spot. With its cracked vinyl seats and 1950s chrome tables, the diner's ambiance was iffy but the food was excellent.

"You remember how I was running around like a chicken with my head cut off trying to find the perfect outfit for a fancy dinner? And how I went online and discovered the restaurant offered a five-hundred-dollar bottle of wine?"

"Don't tell me you guys bought that." Liza didn't bother to apologize for interrupting.

"Not even close. We ended up having chili dogs at the Varsity."

Liza choked on her grits. "The Varsity? As in *the* Varsity."

"Yep."

"This I have to hear."

Maizie told her the whole story including the fact that Clay shook her hand, kissed her on the nose and drove around the block before coming in the back door and heading straight to Hannah's room. He didn't pass Go, he didn't collect his nookie, nothing.

"He wasn't kidding about dating you."

"It appears that way. And it's nice having him around even this much. I just wish he'd talk to me about his work. I know there's still something bothering him."

"So ask him. He's not a mind reader. He's a guy." Liza pointed her fork at Maizie. "You two have never kept secrets before. Why start now?"

"I know." Maizie's shoulders sagged. "But I want him to come to me."

"We don't always get what we want. In this case I think you might have to bite the bullet and go to him. Everything's gonna be okay. I promise, and when have I ever broken a pledge?" Liza picked up her orange juice glass in preparation for a toast.

"To clueless husbands everywhere."

Maizie clinked her glass to her sister's. "To brainless husbands. We can't live with them and we certainly don't plan to live without them."

The twins got a laugh from that. Then Maizie quickly sobered. "I think someone's been in my house."

Liza chewed on her bottom lip. "What makes you think that?"

"Nothing specific. It's just one of those creepy feelings. I bought some imported beer for Clay and I'm almost positive he hasn't had any, but two are missing. A bag of chips is gone and there were crumbs on the family room floor. If Hannah was home I wouldn't think anything of it, but I didn't eat the chips and I don't think Clay did, either. Then there's my underwear drawer."

Liza dropped her fork. "Underwear drawer?"

"I'd bet money someone has been rummaging about in my skivvies. You know how I am about my girly things."

Maizie's obsession with her lingerie was a running joke with the sisters. Everything had to be pristine and in its right place.

"The pinks are on top of the blues."

"Oh, no," Liza gasped in mock consternation. "Not the pinks on top of the blues."

Maizie smacked her sister's arm. "It's not funny. Just the thought of someone putting their hands on my panties gives me chills."

It was Liza's turn to get serious. "I'll let Zack know. I'm sure he'll want to take a look around. Do you mind?"

"I'd appreciate it." Why was someone targeting their house, especially since Clay had moved back home.

"Have you told Clay?"

"Not yet, you're the first. He's going to freak. And if it's only my imagination, I hate to worry him."

CLAY AND HARVEY WERE across town at the DeLite Diner. There was a long-standing debate raging about which establishment had the best grits. As far as Clay was concerned the DeLite won, hands down.

"What's your take on the meeting they had in Atlanta?" Harvey was buttering his biscuit.

"I'm hoping we've finally gotten a break." Most of the trouble they'd been having was due to the unco-operative Department of Transportation planner, and rumor had it there was about to be a shake-up in that office. Apparently it had become obvious to his boss that he was an obstructionist. "If we luck out and get someone reasonable who can work with the construction company, I think we might have a chance. The head honchos at the state want this road built as much as we do. So if luck is on our side, they'll move him to another project. You know how the state feels about firing anyone"

"Yeah, he'll probably get promoted. Whatever, as long as we don't have to deal with him." Harvey wiped his brow. "I pity the poor sucker who gets stuck with him.

"Me, too," Clay replied.

"So what's the latest on the Savannah bid?" Clay asked.

Harvey was taking the lead on preparing a proposal for a highway project in southern Georgia.

"I need to go down there next week and work with our prospective client. I'll be gone three or four days."

"Don't worry about a thing. I can hold down the fort around here."

"Have you told Maizie what we're up against?"

Clay knew his friend was asking out of concern. "Sort of. That's what our big fight was all about. She was upset that I didn't trust her." He thought about their blow-up at the country club. "Actually I'd trust her with my life— I just didn't want to worry her. That was a huge mistake."

Harvey clapped him on the back. "You got that one right. Don't keep anything from your wife. If you do, you're gonna regret it."

Unfortunately that was a lesson that had come home to roost in a big way.

DINNER WAS ANOTHER take-out special—easy and disposable. After cleaning up, Clay and Maizie went to sit on the front porch swing.

It was a cool crisp evening that brought to mind pumpkin pies and falling leaves. "I love this time of year." Maizie pushed the swing back and forth with her foot.

"I love you." Clay leaned over and kissed her. It was as playful as a young crush and a sweet confirmation of a lifelong relationship.

"I know you're mad that I didn't tell you about our problems at work. If I promise to be better will you forgive me?"

He gently rubbed the back of her hand.

"I'm not mad anymore. Really I'm not. My feelings were hurt." She didn't know what else to say.

Clay looked uncomfortable, but what guy wouldn't when stumbling through a heart-to-heart chat. "Since I'm being completely honest, here goes. I think we may be over the worst of this mess." He explained the potential change of leadership at the state level.

Maizie snuggled in closer. "I pray that's the case. But if it isn't, don't worry, we'll make it." She kissed his palm. "All we have to do is stick together."

She was ready to share her suspicion about an intruder when Clay grinned and she was transported back to a time when they were young and desperately in love. Maizie could tell he was about to kiss her, to heck with the nosy neighbors. Then a police car pulled up in front of their house.

Not now!

That irritation dissipated when she saw who was

driving the cruiser. Zack Maynard didn't normally stop by when he was on duty. This couldn't be good.

"Hey guys." Zack walked up on the porch with his hat in hand, literally. "I thought I should come by and talk to you in person." He looked as uneasy as a preacher in a bawdy house.

Clay obviously picked up on the bad vibe. "Let's go inside. From the look on your face, I suspect I'm going to need a drink. Would you like one, Zack?"

"Afraid I can't, not while I'm driving that thing." He pointed at the Crown Vic parked at the curb.

Maizie followed the men inside. "Go on into the kitchen. I'll get us some refreshments."

Zack and Clay sat down at the table while Maizie poured the iced tea and rummaged through the cabinet until she unearthed a package of Oreos. Store-bought cookies weren't company fare, and Mama would be appalled at her pathetic hostess skills, but Maizie suspected this wasn't a social visit.

She placed a glass in front of each man and then took a seat next to her husband. "What's going on, Zack?" Maizie was scared to death she already knew.

"You remember I said I'd come by this morning to give your house a once over. See if there was any sign of someone tampering with a door or whatever."

"Yeah," Maizie said. Her bad feeling was getting even worse.

"There's no easy way to say this, but it appears someone jimmied one of your basement windows."

Maizie's blood ran cold. Someone really had been in her house rummaging through her undies. It hadn't just been her imagination.

Clay didn't say a word. He didn't have to.

"I crawled in and inspected your basement," Zack said. "Have either of you been down there lately?"

"No." Clay's response was clipped.

"How about you?" Zack asked Maizie.

"Not in a couple of weeks." Maizie wondered where he was going with this.

"There are some muddy footprints leading from that window to the stairs. From there I think he took his shoes off."

"Oh, my God!" Maizie's stomach decided to do a barrel roll. "Someone was in this house. Clay, go down and nail all those windows shut." She knew that was like locking the barn door after the horse disappeared, but she was too freaked out to care.

"Why were you checking our windows?" Clay asked. Maizie knew he wouldn't stay quiet long. Not when it was obvious he didn't have all the information.

Zack gave Maizie a curious look. "I think maybe you'd better tell him."

"I suspected someone had been in the house, maybe more than once. Liza said she'd ask Zack to drop by and take a look. I should have told you sooner, but I was afraid it was my imagination. I'm sorry."

Clay was gulping like a fish out of water. "You thought someone had broken in and didn't tell me?" he asked.

Another miscommunication. And this one was entirely her fault. "I didn't want to worry you."

"Worry me! You thought some lunatic had been in our house and you didn't want to worry me!"

Two wrongs didn't make a right, she knew that, but

in this case it was poetic justice. At least that's what she told herself. She took Clay's hand, hoping to keep him from jumping out of his skin.

"I'm sorry. I won't keep any secrets from you again." She managed a lopsided grin. "The worst thing is, I think he rifled around in my lingerie."

"He touched your underwear?" Clay appeared incapable of saying anything without shouting.

Okay, clearly this wasn't the time for jokes.

Zack stood. More than likely he wanted to get the hell away from the two crazy people. "If you want, I can come back tomorrow to do a complete inspection and help you secure the place." He didn't wait for an answer before bolting for the door.

"I'm so sorry, Clay. I should've told you as soon as I thought something was off. From now on, no more secrets." Maizie stuck out her hand. "Deal?"

Clay pulled her into his arms. "Deal."

Were they on the way to healing their marriage and making it even stronger?

"There's something else I need to tell you." Since they were coming clean this was as good a time as any.

Clay stepped away from her and leaned back against the counter.

"What?" he asked, rubbing his forehead.

Maizie chewed on her bottom lip. "You remember when I bought the tennis duds and started taking lessons?"

"Oh, yeah. Vividly."

"There was a little more to it than wanting to get a tan."

Clay didn't say a word.

"I know it was silly, but I thought if you knew someone else found me attractive you'd be jealous. And considering the male population of Magnolia Bluffs, Trip Fitzgerald was the perfect candidate."

Silence.

"It didn't take long to realize that it was one of the most idiotic ideas I'd ever had."

More silence.

"Say something!"

Clay didn't move from his spot against the counter—as far from Maizie as he could get. "What would you like me to say?"

"I don't know. That's funny. What a cute idea. I love you. Any or all of the above." Maizie threw her hands in the air.

To his credit Clay didn't stomp off. He didn't yell, or scream or cuss. He simply rolled his eyes, and that was eloquent enough.

Chapter Twenty-Seven

Liza stopped by Miss Scarlett's Boudoir to see Maizie the next afternoon. "Do you have time to go for coffee?"

Considering folks weren't knocking down the door to spend money Maizie could easily get away.

"Let me tell PJ where I'm going and grab my purse. Check out the new wool slacks. You'd look absolutely darling in them."

"Do you think I could accessorize them with my pearls?"

"Don't you think that would be a mite pretentious?" Maizie asked with a grin.

"Oh, I don't know. Of course I'd have to also wear my tiara."

Maizie's reign as beauty pageant royalty had left her ripe for untold teasing.

"Screw you. Let's get going."

It wasn't until they were walking into the bakery that Liza got to the heart of the matter. "Zack told me you really did have an intruder. Do you have any idea who it might be?"

"Not a clue. Carol and Tim said they saw someone in the woods behind my house. They thought he might be a transient. But in that case, wouldn't he be rummaging through the food rather than my personal things? Though it would explain the chips and beer."

"That sounds logical to me. Can you think of anyone else?"

"Afraid not."

Liza shook her head. "Please, please tell me you're taking precautions."

"I'm being as careful as possible." Maizie patted her purse. "I have my pepper spray with me at all times. Zack and Clay are planning to go through the house with a fine-tooth comb. Hopefully they'll be able to secure the place."

"That's good. You should get an alarm system. I got mine when I was having problems with that homicidal fruitcake and it gave me such peace of mind."

Who could forget the lunatic county council person who had targeted both Liza and Zack?

"Zack has all the information you'd need."

"If I know Clay Walker—and I certainly do—he'll have one ordered before I get home tonight," Maizie said, then paused. "Do you think I should get some protection that's more…" She shrugged, trying to come up with a PC description of a .44 Dirty Harry–type Magnum. "Shall we say, more lethal than a can of pepper spray."

"Do you know how to shoot?" Liza asked, not bothering to disguise her chuckle.

"No."

"Then leave that to the professionals."

"I certainly hope you're not talking about Deputy Bubba."

Liza almost gagged on her chocolate-frosted dough-nut. "No, definitely not Bubba."

Maizie didn't tell Liza that she was seriously con-sidering asking Daddy if she could borrow his shotgun. He always said if you aimed that sucker anywhere near a bad guy, you could do some major damage. "So you wouldn't trust me with a gun, huh?"

"That's a trick question if I ever heard one, and I'm too smart to answer. Here, share my goodie." Liza shoved her half-eaten pastry across the table.

MAIZIE WAS STILL PONDERING security options when Clay walked in the door. She'd cooked him a home-made meal, not that she was buttering him up or anything like that. Considering he hadn't said a word about Trip, she figured good food couldn't hurt.

After he'd stuffed himself on meat loaf, scalloped potatoes and fresh green beans, Maizie popped the question, and she wasn't talking about marriage.

"I'm considering asking Daddy for one of his guns. We could keep it in the bedroom. What do you think?"

CLAY THOUGHT MAIZIE WOULD be a menace with any sort of weapon, but he wasn't about to say so. He valued his body parts too much. "I've made an appoint-ment to get a security system installed."

"Do they really work?"

"Zack thinks so. He said the company I chose is the best around."

Maizie didn't respond, but that didn't necessarily mean she agreed. Clay had been married long enough to know that silence wasn't the same as acceptance. So on to less controversial subject. "How would you like to go for a hayride?"

"A hayride, as in sitting on a bale of hay in a wagon and riding around in the cold?" Maizie asked.

When she put it that way, it did sound lame. But in a moment of weakness at church that Sunday, Clay had told the preacher they'd chaperone the annual Halloween hayride, so it was time for the spin doctor to work his magic.

"It'll be fun. We haven't been on a hayride since we were in the eighth grade."

"Do you think we can neck?"

"With thirty eleven-year-olds watching, I don't think so."

Snuggling, perhaps—actual kissing, not likely. That was best reserved for a soft bed, Egyptian cotton sheets and a warm, willing woman—even if she was the biggest ditz in town.

Clay was still having a hard time coming to grips with her confession. Jealous? Of the pretty-boy tennis pro? Was she kidding? He'd lived with guys ogling her throughout their entire marriage. Sure, the scene at the country club had sent him into a tizzy. Okay, to be completely honest, he'd been so jealous he couldn't see straight. But when he really thought about it, he knew their marriage was rock solid. Cheating wasn't in the cards for either of them.

Actually he thought it was sort of funny but he wasn't about to let Maizie in on that little secret. Let her sweat. That way he'd be getting some good food out of the deal.

Chapter Twenty-Eight

The next day, Maizie was strolling down the toilet paper aisle at the Piggly Wiggly when the hair on the back of her neck stood straight up. She could feel someone was watching her, and swear to God if she caught the jerk she'd bitch-slap him into the next county.

"Let's see," she said loud enough to be heard, "which do I want? The one-ply Piggly Wiggly special or the two-ply softest paper in the world." She picked up a six pack of each and looked back and forth in an amazingly good parody of a toilet paper commercial. She used the opportunity to check out her surroundings. At one end of the aisle she caught a fleeting glimpse of someone with a cart sneaking out of sight.

That did it! If her suspicion was right, and that dirty, low-down lingerie fondler had followed her to the Piggly Wiggly, he was going to be hurtin' for certain. So, with that thought in mind she went on the hunt, up one aisle and down the other, moving with the speed and grace of a cheetah. Out of the way, grannies, the Formula One queen of shopping carts was on the prowl.

No matter how fast she was, the creep was quicker. Maizie would whip around the corner and catch only a momentary impression of a dark-haired man before he disappeared like a puff of smoke. She actually never saw his face, darn it all. However, when she turned onto the produce aisle she hit pay dirt. He had the audacity to be strolling through the bananas—strolling!

"Hey, you!" she yelled, not immediately realizing she'd made her first big mistake.

Without turning to face her, the man ducked behind a huge display of pumpkins. Aha! He was trapped like a rat in a maze. Maizie put her cart in gear and hit the gas—figuratively, that is.

"Ma'am! Ma'am!" The pimply faced stock boy looked as if he'd rather face a firing squad than confront her, but he reached out and grabbed her buggy as she raced by.

"Ma'am," he panted. "What are you doing?"

The overweight manager came running around the corner. "You're disrupting the entire grocery store. We've had so many complaints I can't count them all. I suggest you leave and not come back."

Maizie was *banned* from the Piggly Wiggly. Good golly, Miss Molly, Mama was gonna be apoplectic.

SOMETIMES IT WAS BETTER to break bad news in person. And that was exactly why Maizie had invited Mama, Liza and Kenni to lunch. It would be easier to spill her guts once, rather than doing it over and over again.

Mama was the first to arrive at the tearoom. As usual, she was wearing pearls and a tasteful St. John's outfit.

Before Eleanor sat down she patted Maizie's head. "You're looking a little...peaked."

That was Mama-speak for she looked like something the cat barfed up. Maizie firmly believed that appearances counted, but this time no amount of mascara was going to make any difference. A crazy person was stalking her, and even worse, she'd made a fool of herself in the grocery store.

Maizie put her head in her hands. In the annals of Westerfield history no one had ever been excluded from a retail establishment—that is until she lost her mind and rampaged through the Piggly Wiggly.

"I suppose you've heard."

Of course Mama had, not much got by her, especially when it involved her family.

Liza breezed in and confirmed the worst. "Ohmigod, I just heard the news from Ms. Hightower. Would you like me to sue the Piggly Wiggly?"

Maizie was trying to formulate a pithy comeback when the waitress strolled up and set a plate of chocolate cake topped with whipped cream and chocolate syrup in front of her.

"Miss Violet said you could use this." She pulled a notepad out of her apron and spoke to Mama. "What can I get for you ladies?"

Maizie's initial thought was a new identity, although cake might provide at least temporary relief. Not one to look a gift horse in the mouth, she picked up a fork and dug in.

Kenni was the last to appear, and true to form she wasn't stingy with her affection. The first thing she did was give Maizie a big hug. Considering their height difference, she didn't have to lean down too far.

"Oh, honey. What did you plan to do with him if you caught him?"

Yep, she'd heard, too. Maizie licked chocolate syrup off her lower lip. "I was going to pummel him within an inch of his life and then stuff him in my grocery cart. After that I thought I'd take him to the police station."

Kenni and Liza both broke into laughter. Mama's mirth was a bit more subdued. What would you expect from a charter member of the Magnolia Bluff's Ladies' Book Club?

"Seriously, how could you be so positive it was the guy who broke into your house?" Leave it to Liza to ask the hard question.

"I don't know," Maizie admitted. "I just knew someone was watching me, and when I saw him I knew deep down in my gut he was the guy. Even though he was wearing a baseball cap and sunglasses there was something familiar about him. He had to be the guy I caught on my porch."

"Did you ever consider he might've had a weapon?" Liza had always been the practical twin.

The answer was a resounding no. At the time Maizie had been running on adrenaline. She hadn't thought much past the delight of cramming him into her cart.

"I suppose I would've been in a mess of trouble," she admitted.

"I'm afraid you're right," Liza concurred.

"Maizie girl, please promise you won't pull a stunt like that again."

Mama looked vulnerable—and that was truly amazing.

WHEN MAIZIE GOT HOME there were two step vans parked out front, both bearing signs indicating they belonged to Atlanta's Best Alarms. Men with tool belts were scurrying about.

Maizie had nearly made it through the gauntlet of workers when Clay pulled into the drive. "I suppose you heard about the brouhaha in the produce aisle," she stated as he climbed out of the truck. Of course he had. Otherwise there wouldn't be an army of handymen wiring every door and window in the house. Clay had probably paid a premium for a rush job.

"It's the talk of the town." Clay held up a sack from the Piggly Wiggly delicatessen and walked with her into the kitchen. "I brought dinner." He had the gall to laugh. "I can still go to the grocery store."

"That's not funny."

"It is to me," he said with another chuckle.

Clay put the sack on the table and took her in his arms. "Seriously, I want you to promise me that if you see this nut again you'll call Zack."

That was a no-brainer. The Piggly Wiggly fiasco had been a huge mistake.

"Okay, I promise."

"The guys are going to work until they finish. We're not spending another night in this house without an alarm."

Maizie couldn't fault his reasoning. After everything that had happened, an alarm sounded like a fantastic idea.

"Did you talk to Zack?" Maizie grabbed a bottle of iced tea from one of the bags and went out to the front porch.

Clay joined her on the swing. "I did, and he's as frustrated as we are."

"There has to be something else we can do, or Zack can do, or God can do."

"I'm afraid not, at least not for us mortals. I don't think I can speak for God." Clay chuckled. "I won't let anyone hurt you." He pulled Maizie onto his lap and tucked her head under his chin. "If he wants to get to you, he's gonna have to go through me."

"Don't say that!"

Clay tilted her chin to look her in the eye. "It's true."

Chapter Twenty-Nine

The rest of the week was quiet—no intruders, no strange cars lurking around, no disturbed underwear drawer, absolutely nothing. That was just fine. Maizie was fed up with the drama.

The weekend and the dreaded hayride came about much faster than expected. Maizie didn't mind wearing a Halloween costume. That wasn't the problem. Her funk had more to do with the overall state of her marriage.

Yes, it was much improved, but even though Clay swore he'd protect her with his life, he hadn't returned to their bed. And darn it, she was horny as all heck!

Then there was the matter of her stalker. Now that they had an alarm she was fairly confident he couldn't paw through her Victoria's Secret goodies. However, she still had the feeling someone was watching her. She'd shared that concern with Clay but there wasn't much more he could do. He was already glued to her hip. So really, what could happen to her with him around all the time?

Occasionally, Maizie had seen the same car driving

up and down the street in front of the Boudoir. She forced herself not to worry about it. After all, she couldn't report some forgetful little old lady making repeated trips to the drugstore.

Darn, this situation made her mad. Magnolia Bluffs had always been a safe place. A community where you could raise your kids, and live your life and grow old without constantly thinking about crime. It wasn't necessary to lock your doors unless you wanted to teach your husband a lesson. You didn't have to worry about walking down the street alone, and you certainly didn't have to wire your house like Fort Knox. The good times, however, were apparently in the past.

"What are you going to do for a costume?" PJ asked as they stocked the racks the afternoon before the hayride. She'd been privy to Maizie's minor angst concerning the kid party.

"I can't use my Marilyn Monroe outfit. It's too racy. And I don't think the witch costume will go over well with the preacher. A couple of folks in the church have this thing about witchcraft and Satan. So I'm stuck."

"You guys could team up. How about doing Laurel and Hardy or Annie Oakley and Wild Bill Hickok?"

Maizie briefly considered PJ's suggestions before dismissing both ideas. "That's too much work. I need something quick and easy."

"Hmm, quick and easy. Let me think." PJ put her finger on her cheek as though that would help the ideas come.

And that's how Clay and Maizie ended up going to the party dressed as Casper the Friendly Ghost and his friend Casperette. You couldn't get much easier than cutting eye holes into a couple of sheets.

"I feel like an unmade bed," Clay griped as he tried to drink hot cider without soaking his costume.

"Don't complain to me. The hayride wasn't my idea." Although she'd been far from enthusiastic about it in the beginning, Maizie was having fun.

What was it about a Halloween party that appealed to her inner kid? She couldn't decide whether it was the caramel apples, the popcorn balls or the sugar cookies iced like pumpkins that excited her. Or perhaps it was the children's exuberance that made it so much fun.

The party was delightful. The hayride was...well... not so much. Thanks to a cold front the temperature had dropped below freezing. It gave new meaning to the phrase putting the frost on the pumpkin—and the tip of her nose.

"I feel like the Michelin Man," Maizie complained. She was wearing a down parka under her Casperette sheet. "And my feet are freezing."

"Let's get cozy." Clay drew her into his warmth.

"That feels good." Maizie savored not only his body heat but also his closeness. "I suppose kissing is still out, huh?"

Clay gave her the lopsided grin she loved so much. "'Fraid so. We have a bunch of little eyes on us." He indicated the assembled group of eleven-year-olds.

"Can you imagine how fast that would hit the grapevine?" Clay ratcheted his smile up a notch.

Chaperones necking on a church hayride—yep, that would definitely be the talk of the town.

BY SUNDAY AFTERNOON Maizie was still smarting over the fact that nothing had happened even after they got home. She understood Clay's logic about chaperone decorum, truly she did, but how could he stand in the front hall and kiss her senseless, and then calmly stroll to Hannah's bedroom, leaving her alone and stewing.

And speaking of stew, post-church lunch at Mama's was a semi-mandatory appearance, not that Maizie usually minded. Who could resist meat that could melt in your mouth, butter beans, homemade yeast rolls and bacon spinach salad? And don't forget the chocolate meringue pie. It was to die for.

Liza, Maizie and Mama were in the sunroom having a glass of sweet tea while the guys were engrossed in a Falcons football game.

"How was the hayride?" Mama asked.

"Cold."

"Cold? You mean you didn't get all cuddled up with your honey?" Liza asked.

Maizie threw a napkin at her twin. "Not so you could tell."

"Girls, girls. Swear to goodness, I'm not sure you two are ever going to grow up." Mama tempered her criticism with an affectionate smile that quickly turned somber. "Let's talk about your Piggly Wiggly encounter. Have you seen the guy lately?"

"No, but I keep looking." Maizie ran her fingers through her hair. "Every once in a while I find myself jumping at my own shadow."

"I still can't believe you chased him through the grocery store," Eleanor said. "Heavens to Betsy, you could have been hurt. What *am* I going to do with you?"

Liza jabbed her sister. "Yeah, what *is* she going to do with you?" This was a familiar refrain from Mama.

The year before Liza had been pursued by a serial killer.

"At least this guy is only fondling my panties, he's not shooting at me," Maizie retorted, then laughed thinking about a grown man seeking refuge behind a stack of pumpkins. "You really should've seen me with that cart. I could qualify for NASCAR."

"Believe me, I heard all about it." Mama fanned herself. "That was so dangerous."

At the time Maizie hadn't considered the consequences of confronting her stalker. The dude had to be crazy. Otherwise, why would he be pawing through her panties? So why hadn't she dialed 911 instead of racing through the canned goods like Dale Earnhardt Jr.?

Maizie grabbed her mom's hand. "I won't do anything like that again, I promise." She crossed her heart, and this time she really meant it. But truth be told, she'd give a hundred bucks for just five minutes with the idiot who was making her life a nightmare. Before she got through with him, he'd be crying uncle. Damned straight, he would.

Maizie was still contemplating the possibilities when Clay sat down next to her on the chintz couch.

"Is the game over?"

"Nope, it's halftime." Clay put his arm around Maizie. "I need to ask Liza for a favor."

"You name it and you've got it." Liza was apparently in an agreeable mood.

"Harvey just called. He was supposed to go to Savannah to meet with a new client but Sarah ended up in the hospital."

"She's in the hospital? What happened?" Maizie asked quickly. Sarah was one of her favorite people.

"She had to have emergency gallbladder surgery. Harvey said she's going to be fine. The doctors want to keep her a couple of days so he has to stay home with the kids."

It took a moment for the realization to dawn. Clay had to go to Savannah. "You're leaving town?"

"I won't be gone long." He turned his attention back to Liza. "That's the favor I'd like to ask. Would you stay with Maizie until I get back? Zack said he'll be working nights, but he'll check in on you two when he can."

"Count me in. We'll have a slumber party. Right, sis?" Liza punched Maizie on the arm in a lifelong gesture of affection. "When do you leave?" she asked.

"Tomorrow morning."

"Hey, Maze. What are you making me for dinner?"

Maizie threw a pillow at her sister. "Haven't you heard I've been banned from our purveyor of fine groceries? What do you suppose they have at the Stop and Shop?" she asked sweetly. "We can always have Cheetos and Dr Pepper."

"Fine. I'll bring dinner," Liza said with a grin.

Chapter Thirty

A day later, Eleanor was having lunch with her sisters, Anna Belle and Eugenie. In their heyday, the Carpenter sisters had been the terrors of Magnolia Bluffs County—not that Eleanor would admit that to her own daughters.

"I'm worried about the girls spending the night in Maizie's house without a man," Eleanor said, knowing Anna Belle and Eugenie would understand her concern.

Although the Carpenter sisters had moved with the times, they still held some old-fashioned Southern convictions, namely that men were handy to have around. To their way of thinking a guy was good at opening jars, getting rid of spiders, moving furniture and, best of all, scaring the bejeezus out of intruders.

"What do you have in mind?" Anna Belle asked. She was the least daring of the trio. Even in her sixties, she still looked like she could sing in a choir of angels.

Eugenie was the athletic sister, and although she'd been married to a lawman for decades, she was never one to back away from an adventure.

Eugenie took a healthy bite of a buttered roll. "What are you thinking, Ellie?"

Eleanor leaned forward and lowered her voice. "I want to revive our Nancy Drew club."

Eugenie and Anna Belle looked at each other before bursting into gales of laughter.

"Are you serious?" Eugenie asked. "We're not exactly spring chickens, or haven't you noticed?"

Eleanor waved off her comment. "Don't be silly. You're only as old as you feel."

"Let's discuss this logically." Anna Belle had always been the peacemaker of the group. "What are you suggesting we do?"

"I think we should keep an eye on Maizie's house at night. Zack plans to cruise by every hour, but in between anything could happen." Eleanor shuddered.

Rascal that she was, Eugenie had the twinkle in her eye that meant she was interested. "So how would *we* keep an eye on the house?"

"Do you remember the tree house Clay built for Hannah?"

Anna Belle's expression softened. "That reminds me of the playhouse Joe built for the girls. Do you recall the summer Liza, Maizie and Kenni spent most of their time in our backyard?"

Anna Belle had adopted Kenni when she was a little girl and she'd been an integral part of the extended Carpenter family ever since.

Eleanor remembered it like it was yesterday, but she couldn't afford to be distracted. "So back to the tree house. Do you think the floor is still intact?"

"Spit it out, Eleanor. What's your brilliant idea?" Eugenie asked.

"This. We can spend the night in the tree house and

keep an eye on the girls." The tree house was perfectly situated in an ancient magnolia in the side yard and had a great view of both the front and back doors.

Eugenie hesitated, but then made up her mind. "I'm in."

"Me, too," Anna Belle agreed. "That's what family is for. So what's the game plan?"

Eleanor knew she could count on her sisters—they simply had to give her a hard time first. "We have to start tonight. I'll need your help getting everything set up."

"What should we tell the men? Dave will have a fit if he gets wind of this." Eugenie's husband had been the sheriff for years. He'd recently retired and helped Zack get elected.

"I'm going to tell Bennett we made a last-minute decision to go to the coast for a church retreat."

"I'm not sure lying about God is a good idea," Anna Belle offered.

Eleanor suspected that if her sister had been Catholic she would've been crossing herself. As it was, she had to make do with crossing her fingers.

"Why don't we tell them we're going an overnight shopping spree in Savannah? Joe would believe that," Anna Belle said.

"So would Dave."

"That works for me," Eleanor agreed. "I'll pick you guys up later this afternoon. We can have dinner and hang out until it gets good and dark. I'm heading into Atlanta today to buy some supplies."

"What kind of supplies are we talking about?" Eugenie was getting into the spirit of the adventure.

"I thought I'd look for some night-vision goggles and other covert ops equipment."

Eugenie clapped her hands; she was definitely in. Anna Belle was a bit more iffy, but she'd come around. She'd have to be on her death bed to miss a party.

"IT'S SO DARK I CAN'T see my hand in front of my face," Anna Belle whispered. Stealth was the name of the game as the Carpenter sisters hauled their gear across Maizie's lawn.

"And this cooler weighs a ton. What do you have in here?" Eugenie moaned.

"Shh. The girls are still awake." Eleanor indicated the lights in the family room and kitchen. "We have to be very quiet."

That put a stop to the sisters' conversation until they reached the base of the magnolia tree and realized exactly what they were facing.

"How do we get this stuff up there?" Eugenie pointed at the platform twenty feet in the air.

That was a good question. How *did* they get twenty pounds of equipment up a tree without breaking a hip, alerting the girls or getting arrested?

"I'll climb up with the rope and tie it off. Then you can attach it to the cooler and all that other stuff," Anna Belle offered. She was the smallest sister, and therefore the best one to test the strength of the floor.

"Okay, go for it." Eugenie gave her sister a boost so she could reach the first rung.

"It's hard to see the stupid steps," Anna Belle hissed. By that time she was almost halfway up the tree. "If I break my neck I'm going to haunt you forever. You just wait."

Oops—Anna Belle didn't make idle threats.

An eternity—or probably only minutes—later, Eleanor and Eugenie heard her call down to them. "I'm up. Watch out I'm going to lower the rope."

A lot of good the warning did, Eleanor thought when the knot hit her on the head.

It took almost twenty minutes to haul up their treasure trove consisting of surveillance equipment, Diet Cokes and an air mattress. They were working on the theory of why be uncomfortable. And they were making so much noise it was a wonder they hadn't roused the entire neighborhood.

"That about did me in." Anna Belle was breathing so hard she could barely speak. "It's not nearly as much fun as when we were kids."

"Hey, sis, I have a news flash. We're not kids anymore," Eugenie whispered. "My knee is killing me and I'm not sure I can get down."

"Hush!" Eleanor put her finger to her lips and pointed at the front porch light. "They heard us. Hunker down."

"DID YOU HEAR SOMETHING?" Maizie asked as she refilled Liza's wineglass.

"I don't think so." Liza paused the Pay-for-View movie they were watching and cocked her head. "Nope, I don't hear a thing."

"I could've sworn I heard giggling. That's weird. I'll just run out and check." Maizie set aside her bowl of popcorn.

Liza pulled herself up off the floor. "Not by yourself

you're not. We'll both go. If there's anyone out there, we'll call Zack." She held up her cell phone. "I have him on speed dial."

Maizie flipped on the front and back porch lights before grabbing her emergency flashlight. "Are you ready?"

"Let's go." Liza pushed her sister toward the door.

"Why don't you go first?"

"You're bigger."

"And you're meaner," Maizie retorted. "Oh shoot, get behind me." The Westerfield twins tiptoed in tandem out onto the front porch.

"Do you see anything?" Maizie asked as she swung the light in an arch from the street to Carol and Tim's hedge.

Liza peeked out from around her sister. "Not a thing."

"Chicken." Maizie clucked. "Okay, Chicken Little, come on inside. We'll go out back and see if there's anything's there."

"I should have brought P.B. He'd at least bark if someone came up on the porch." P.B.—short for Peanut Butter—was Liza's golden retriever. That silly dog would treat an intruder like a long-lost buddy.

"Jelly Belly would be better," Maizie said. "At least he could latch on to his heel." Jelly Belly was Liza's toy poodle and P.B.'s best friend.

"Yeah, yeah. Come on." Liza grabbed the hem of Maizie's T-shirt and pulled her back inside. "Standing in the light makes us perfect targets."

Maizie hadn't thought of that. She followed her twin to the back door and flipped off the porch light.

"Is that better?"

"I think so," Liza agreed as they stepped outside.

After repeating the procedure of shining the flashlight into every nook and cranny of the yard and finding nothing, Maizie and Liza retreated to the safety of the house.

"Is the alarm on?" Liza asked.

"I just re-armed it. According to the guys who installed it, a flea couldn't get in here without us knowing it. I certainly hope they're right."

"Me, too." Liza resumed her reclining position on the couch. "Should I call Zack?"

"I don't know. What do you think?"

"We didn't see anything and we didn't hear anyone. I'd hate to drag him over here for nothing."

Chapter Thirty-One

"That was close." Eleanor breathed a sigh of relief. "I'm glad they didn't catch us, but it worries me they didn't check the side yard. They're already suspicious so we really have to be quiet."

"Yeah," Eugenie agreed as the Carpenter girls settled in for a long stakeout.

An hour later all was quiet in the neighborhood, and even though the light was still on in the family room there wasn't a sound coming from Maizie's house.

"I think I hear a car." Eugenie sat up. The sisters had been resting on the air mattress.

"It's probably that Brent Hardwick coming home from a bar," Anna Belle whispered. "What kind of behavior is that for a church deacon, I ask you."

She poked her head up over the rail. "Oh, dear. Whoever it is has turned off the headlights and rolled past the Hardwick house. Do you think we have our perp?" Anna Belle was sounding less enthusiastic by the minute.

Eleanor popped up to see for herself. Sure enough, a sedan drove slowly down the street—too slowly for any legitimate purpose. "If that's not suspicious, I'll pay for lyin'."

The Carpenter sisters' original idea was to call the cops the minute anyone questionable stepped on Maizie's property. Like so many best-laid plans, there was a glitch.

"I'm not getting a signal," Eugenie hissed. She smacked her cell as if that would make a couple of bars magically appear.

Eleanor grabbed the phone. "Give me that thing." She peered at the screen, hoping her sister was just too technologically challenged to make it work. "How did that happen? We had service when we were on the ground."

"It's probably all these leaves." Eugenie swatted away some of the lustrous green offenders. "I think they're interfering with the reception."

"I guess that means we're on our own," Eleanor muttered, not quite sure she had anything in her toolbox of crime-fighting skills to handle this situation. Not to worry—steel magnolias were known for the ability to adapt.

"Line up a whole bunch of Cokes," Eleanor told Anna Belle. "Genie, how's your pitching arm?"

Back when they were kids, Eugenie had been a star slow-pitch player. "Not as good as it used to be, but I might be able to hit something, or someone, if that's the idea."

"That's exactly the idea."

As the car rolled by and rounded the corner the ladies got ready. Soon, their patience paid off. A figure dressed all in black came slinking across the Templetons' yard.

"Is that a man?" Anna Belle whispered.

"I don't know. Kind of looks like it, but with the ski mask, I really can't tell," Eugenie answered.

"He's definitely up to no good. It's time for a good old-fashioned ass whoopin'." And Eleanor Westerfield was the girl to do it.

The intruder got down on all fours and crawled toward the back porch, oblivious to the fact that he was about to encounter the Magnolia Bluffs version of Charlie's Angels.

"He's up on the porch. I can't tell what he's doing," Anna Belle whispered. She was watching him through the night-vision goggles. The ladies of the church league would pop their garters if they saw her.

"Keep an eye on him," Eugenie instructed. "If he gets the door open, we're gonna have to blast him."

Anna Belle had lined up at least a dozen soft drink cans. At the end of that arrangement Eleanor had placed a high-powered flashlight. They were ready for anything.

"Oh, goodness! He broke the window," Anna Belle squealed.

But her sisters could hardly hear her over the blast of the alarm. It was loud enough to be heard in downtown Atlanta.

"Good Lord!" Maizie screamed. The alarm sounded like the hounds of hell had been set loose.

"Someone's trying to break in," Liza screeched. She frantically punched numbers into her cell.

Maizie grabbed her pepper spray and a fireplace poker. Why had she let Clay talk her out of borrowing Daddy's shotgun?

"Get down behind the couch." Liza grabbed Maizie's hand and yanked her to the floor. The strength adrenaline could give such a small person was amazing.

"Zack's on his way and he's bringing the cavalry. And I have this." Liza rummaged through her purse and pulled out a stun gun. "It's cop regulation."

Although Maizie could hear only about a third of what her sister was saying, the stun gun said it all.

"HE'S RUNNING. HIT THE LIGHT, Anna Belle. Get your throwin' arm ready, Eugenie!" The over-sixty crew went on an all-out assault. Eleanor prepared for a soda can assault.

"He's coming this way!" Eugenie grabbed a couple of cans ready to at least slow him down.

"Wait, wait." Eleanor was the commanding officer on the ops. "Now, Genie, now!" The prowler was obviously disoriented by the hullabaloo. He ran first one way, then another and then he ran straight toward his enemies.

Eugenie hadn't thrown a ball in years, but like riding a bike, it was a skill that returned with a vengeance. Bingo—the first can hit him on the top of the head.

"Good going!" Eleanor screamed. "Keep it up!"

After her initial success, the Nolan Ryan wannabe pummeled the intruder with can after can of Diet Coke. When he tried to protect his head, she'd aim for his back, his butt, or the ground in front of him. The cans popped open, spraying sticky soda everywhere. It was a mess, but it was also a glorious victory.

Lights were coming on all over the neighborhood. A siren wailed in the distance and the intruder crashed through the Templetons' hedge before disappearing into the darkness.

"How do we get down from here?" Anna Belle asked as she looked toward the ground.

ZACK'S CRUISER SCREECHED to a halt just as Maizie and Liza raced out the front door, each carrying their weapon of choice.

Liza threw herself into her husband's arms.

"Darlin'." Zack gave her a quick kiss and set her aside. "I have to find out what's happening."

His radio crackled to attention. "Sheriff, there's a report of someone stealing a car on the next street over."

"Get a couple of units on it. I'll look around here," he told his deputy. "And you two—" he pointed at Liza and Maizie "—stay right where you are. Don't move." A second police car arrived and more officers spilled out.

Maizie wasn't about to stand on the porch while the big dogs did their thing. She followed Zack to the tree and glanced up, Liza close behind.

Maizie was blown away by what she saw. "Mother! *What* are you doing?"

"Trying to get down, dear. But Anna Belle's too slow."

Auntie Anna Belle was halfway down the ladder. Eleanor's ample rump was barely visible and Aunt Eugenie was peering over the rail.

Zack plucked Anna Belle off the last rung. "Eleanor, do you want me to help you down?"

"No, honey. Just get out of the way. I'd hate to make my daughter a widow again."

Zack was trying admirably to hold in his laughter, though Maizie could tell it was a mighty effort.

Liza poked her husband in the ribs. "It's not funny."

"It isn't? Are you sure?"

By the time the three ladies were on terra firma, Zack had himself under control. "Would someone please tell me what happened?"

"We—" Anna Belle started to speak but she was interrupted by her sister.

"He—" Eugenie said.

"We're protecting our babies," Eleanor finished. "That man broke the glass and was about to open the door."

Zack glanced at the house before issuing some instructions. "Stay right here. I'll go check it out." He stalked to the back door.

"What in the world did you think you were doing?" Maizie was so astonished she could barely speak.

Liza picked up one of the cans. "You bombarded him with Diet Cokes?" she asked. "That's…that's…hilarious." Liza was laughing so hard she had tears in her eyes.

Maizie stared at her twin. The doofus had gone over the edge. Then she took a good look at the matriarchs of the family. Unbelievable! Now that the immediate danger had passed, she had to admit it was pretty funny. Or perhaps that was hysteria talking.

The entire neighborhood was assembled on Maizie's front lawn, forcing Zack's officers to act as crowd control.

Zack radioed Bubba. "Have you found anyone over there?"

"Not yet, boss. The report of the stolen car was nothing more than some guy sneaking out after a…a…"

Zack took pity on his deputy's apparently delicate sensibilities. "A tryst?"

"Yeah, that's it. Anyway, a man on the next block saw a silver Honda parked a couple of doors down from his house but he didn't think it was important enough to get a license number."

"That's great, just freakin' fantastic," Zack muttered.

Maizie pointed at the lawn scattered with soda cans. "The idiot didn't stand a chance against the Carpenter sisters. They were about to take him out," she said with more than a little admiration.

Zack turned his frown on the Carpenter sisters. "Did you ever consider he might be armed?"

"Umm, no, I hadn't thought of that," Eleanor admitted.

"And what did you think he was planning to do once he got in the house?"

"I don't know."

Zack took his wife's hand. "I'm tempted to run you ladies in," he said shaking his head.

"Oh, come on," Maizie exclaimed. "I agree, they're nuts, but they were trying to protect us. And if you ran Aunt Eugenie in, Sheriff Dave would have your hide." Maizie didn't bother to hide her grin. When she was right, she was right.

Chapter Thirty-Two

It was the middle of the night and Clay was sound asleep, having a very nice dream. That ended abruptly when his cell blasted out the "William Tell Overture."

"Hello?" he muttered, trying to clear his throat.

"Oh, Clay. Mama…Mama…she." Maizie was either sobbing or hiccupping—he couldn't decide which— and then the call was dropped. What in hell was happening?

He turned on the bedside light and looked at the display on his phone. His battery was dead.

Clay grabbed the hotel phone, dialed his home number and was immediately sent to voice mail.

"Maizie, I'm on my way. My phone's dead but I'll try to find a pay phone along the road. I'll be there as soon as I can."

He threw on a pair of jeans and a T-shirt before dumping everything else into his suitcase. The client would have to wait. He'd make amends for missing tomorrow's meeting when he got home. The important thing was making sure Maizie was all right.

Clay made the three-hour trip in just over two

hours—and yep, he'd broken every traffic law on the books. The sun was starting to rise as he pulled into the drive.

The house hadn't burned down—thank heavens. Maizie's car was in the driveway—that was a positive sign. But why were there Coke cans all over the lawn? The scene was awfully similar to of one of his college frat parties.

At first glance, things seemed fairly normal—except for the kegger look. But that was before he noticed Zack's cruiser parked across the street. Oh, crap. Why hadn't he stayed home?

Clay was out of the car and in the back door like a shot.

"Mary Stuart Walker, where are you?"

Halfway up the stairs he encountered his brother-in-law and grabbed his arm.

"What happened?" Clay wanted answers and he wanted them immediately.

By that time, both Maizie and Liza had joined the men on the landing.

"Clay, what are you doing here?" His wife had the audacity to look puzzled.

He took a deep breath, as much to lower his blood pressure as to keep from screaming. "You called me last night hysterical about your mother. What did you expect me to do, roll over and go back to sleep?" Clay realized he was shouting but he couldn't help himself.

"Oh, sweetie," Maizie said with a smile. "I wasn't hysterical, I was laughing. You won't believe what Mama and my aunts did last night."

She thought it was funny that he'd almost killed

himself driving hell-bent-to-leather to come to her rescue? It was so amusing he'd almost had a coronary. It was so funny…forget it. His righteous indignation took a nosedive in the face of his exhaustion. Not to mention he was so hungry he could eat an elephant.

"I'm going to fix breakfast," he grumped. "Who wants to join me?" It was more of a command than an invitation.

After a meal of strawberry waffles and hot coffee Clay wiped his mouth and glared at his wife. "What happened? And don't leave out a thing." She had to know he'd get any missing information from Zack.

After Maizie and Liza finished their narrative, periodically interrupting each other, Clay had a clear mental picture of what had gone down. While he had to admit that his mother-in-law's participation was side-splitting—he hadn't known she had it in her—the fact that someone almost got in the house made his blood run cold. Thank God they had an alarm.

Clay glanced at his brother-in-law the sheriff. He hadn't contributed much to the story. "Who do you think it was?"

"I don't know. The intruder was long gone before we arrived," Zack said. "Maizie doesn't have any enemies that we know of. Is there anyone who has it in for you?"

Clay was desperate for a shower and a couple hours' sleep. "I can't think of a soul who'd want to hurt us. Obviously we're missing a piece of this puzzle. Now we have to figure out what it is."

"I'm going to increase the number of patrols we do on this block, but just between us, I'd suggest you get a gun. Not that I'm telling you to do anything rash. Now I'm going back to the station to put out some feelers. Maybe one of our neighboring jurisdictions has run into the same MO." Zack turned to his wife. "Come on, darlin'. I'll take you home."

Liza didn't resist. She had her bag in her hand. "I'm right behind you."

Maizie hugged her sister. "Thanks for keeping me company." She grinned. "You have to admit it was entertaining."

"It certainly was."

Clay and Maizie walked the Hendersons to the door and waved goodbye.

"I have to call Harvey and tell him I'm staying in town." Although work was important, Clay didn't intend to leave his wife's side. One of his young engineers would have to take over the Savannah project, at least for the time being.

"I'm not letting you out of my sight, at least not until we can make heads or tails of all this."

"I'm scared." That was the first time Maizie had admitted it out loud. "It's the fear of the unknown that's making me crazy." She couldn't quite verbalize what she was feeling. It almost felt as if the guy had the ability to disappear at will.

Maizie was a true crime junkie so she knew many women had faced this unbelievably terrifying situation. She simply never thought she'd be one of them.

Clay pulled Maizie close. "The guy's a sicko. We'll find him, I promise."

"I know that up here." She touched her head and then placed her hand over her heart. "But here, where it counts, I'm scared. None of this makes any sense. Why would someone stalk us? We're plain folks. Why would he be interested in us?"

Clay answered by tilting her chin and pressing his lips to hers. It was an erotic journey home. It started out soft and sweet, then quickly turned into a kiss of the soul, hot and carnal. It was a confirmation of love, friendship, commitment and everything that was wonderful about their relationship.

"Does this mean you're moving back into our bedroom?" Maizie asked when they finally came up for air.

"What do you think?" Clay pulled her T-shirt over her head and discarded it on the living room floor. Then he traced his fingers up her back to pop open the clasp of her bra.

"I remember the first time you did that. Do you?"

"Uh-huh. Now hush." Clay slid his hands to her midriff, and proceeded to gently massage her nipples. This was heaven. This was how it was supposed to be. This was perfect.

Slowly, inch by inch, kiss by sensual kiss, Maizie slid back on the couch cushions until Clay was leaning over her, murmuring sweet nothings and doing even sweeter things to her body.

Chapter Thirty-Three

Maizie was having a "whoa, mama" dream when she suddenly awoke. At first she was annoyed that she'd missed the punch line, but when she opened her eyes, she realized reality was better than any dream.

Clay was where he was supposed to be—right by her side. She thanked her lucky stars when he rolled over and gave her the same sexy smile she'd loved for nearly three decades.

"Hey, sweetheart." Clay put his arm around her waist and pulled her to his chest. "How are you feeling this morning?"

Clay and Maizie's previous afternoon had segued from fantastic make-up loving, to an erotic dinner of strawberries and whipped cream, on to a stimulating shower, and then back to bed.

"Fantastic. I'd love to stay here all day." She rubbed against him like an affectionate kitten.

"I would, too. Regrettably, we both have to go to work. You know, to make money. Pay the mortgage. Keep the kid in college. Stuff like that."

"I know." She couldn't resist a sly grin. "We have

thirty minutes. What do you think we can get done in that time?"

"Debate the upcoming city council election?"

The silly man was begging for a smack. Instead she gave his chest hair a friendly tweak.

"That does it." He rolled her over on her back for a replay of the previous evening.

And that's how they spent the next thirty minutes.

MAIZIE WAS ON HER second waffle when Clay finally made it downstairs. He was showered, shaved and too handsome for words.

He sat down and pilfered a bite of her waffle. "I'm taking you to the boutique and then I have to run by the office for a while. We have some damage control to do on the Savannah project. I'm hoping that today we'll get some good news about that infamous interchange."

"Do you think everything's going to be okay?" For Clay's sake she prayed the situation would work out. If it didn't, that would be all right, too. As long as they had their family, everything else was gravy.

"I hope so. We're about to find out. I'll come back to the Boudoir as soon as I can get away. Promise me you won't go anywhere by yourself. This guy is getting gutsier by the day."

Maizie twined her fingers through his. "Don't worry about me. I'll be in a public place and PJ will be there. If anything should go wrong I have Zack's number on the speed dial. He promised he'd come running."

"I know." Clay chuckled. "Humor me. It'll make me feel better."

"Okay, I promise I won't leave the shop unless you're with me."

CLAY WAS IN THE MIDDLE of a conference call when Janice, his receptionist, came in and signaled that he had another call.

"It's important," she mouthed. "Really important."

Clay's stomach flip-flopped. "I'm sorry," he interrupted the speaker. "I have a family emergency. I have to leave this with you guys." He hung up, hoping to God he was overreacting.

"What is it, Janice?"

"The sheriff's on the phone. He said it was urgent." Janice obviously wanted to stick around. "Do you need anything else from me?"

"No, that's it. Thanks."

"Oh, okay." She reluctantly took her leave.

What was wrong now? Clay connected to Zack's call. "What's up?" He didn't bother with any preliminaries.

"I have some news that you're not going to like."

"I NEED TO GO TO the post office. I'll be back in fifteen minutes or less, I promise," PJ said, making an elaborate display of crossing her heart.

"Don't worry. I've been alone in this shop thousands of times. I'm not afraid. Go." Maizie made a shooing motion with her hands. Trip Fitzgerald came in as PJ was leaving.

"Hi, Trip. Are you shopping again? You certainly

have lucky relatives." PJ held the door open for the tennis pro.

"Yep, it's my sister's birthday this time. Can you stick around to help me?"

PJ blushed to the roots of her curly do. "I would, but I have to get this in today's mail." She held up an envelope. "I'll have to pay interest on my credit card if I don't." The smile she gave him was far too flirtatious for a married mother of two.

"Maizie will be glad to help you. See ya." She threw him a cheeky three-finger wave.

Maizie listened to the banter between PJ and Trip.

"Hi, Trip," she greeted him warmly. It was nice to see a friendly face. "I haven't talked to you in ages."

"I'm still at the country club. We've missed you at the lessons." He grinned before getting serious. "I've heard what's been happening. It's terrible."

"Things have been crazy around here lately," Maizie admitted as she straightened the rack of blouses, arranging things according to size and color.

As much as she liked Trip, she didn't think it was appropriate to spill her guts to him.

"Do you want to tell me about it?"

Somehow he'd managed to move much closer than Maizie expected, so she sidestepped, trying to get out of his way. Didn't he understand the importance of personal space?

"I'm certain the sheriff will find the guy soon." When she moved to the other side of the carousel, he followed, step for step. His behavior was giving her the creeps. Was she being too sensitive or was there really something off here?

Maizie plastered on her best shopkeeper smile. "So, what can I help you with today?"

He didn't answer, but he did glance around as if he was looking for something, or someone. "Are you alone?"

On the surface the question seemed innocent. All the same, Maizie's intuition went on high alert. PJ had said she'd back in fifteen minutes, but knowing her she'd make a side trip by the bookstore or the Dairy Queen or the nail salon.

Maizie couldn't put her finger on what was making her nervous, but it was better to err on the side of caution. After all, she'd promised Clay. That meant she needed to keep Trip talking and distracted so she could get behind the counter to the phone.

"No. As a matter of fact Clay is unloading some boxes in the store room."

Trip's smile was worthy of a snake-oil salesman. Why hadn't she noticed his smarminess before now?

Red flags were waving all over the place. Maizie eased the cordless off its base. Please God, she was being unreasonable. She'd much rather be embarrassed than dead. Could Trip Fitzgerald be her stalker?

She got her answer when he snatched the phone out of her hand.

"What are you doing?" Maizie squeaked. When the going got rough she always seemed to turn into Minnie Mouse.

"I don't think you want to call anyone."

Chills skittered up her spine. "Why are you here?"

"I told you. I'm shopping." His voice was so cold it sent the temperature plunging.

"I don't believe you."

Why had she ever thought he had nice eyes? At the moment they seemed more reptilian than human. And then it hit her—no white knight was going to ride to her rescue, not even Clay. Maizie had never felt so alone.

Chapter Thirty-Four

Clay made it to Zack's office in record time.

"Why don't you sit down and have a cup of coffee." Zack indicated the coffeemaker on his credenza.

It was a classic stall but Clay decided to play along, at least for a few minutes. "I'm not desperate enough to drink that stuff." He shuddered. "What time did you make it?"

"Yesterday."

"Enough said. So, what's the information you found?" he asked, not willing to wait a second longer.

Zack leaned back in his leather chair. "I had one of my detectives check sex-offender registries all over the South. We didn't find anything there, but when he did a statewide search on stalker cases, he came up with several that looked similar, and they were all attached to the same person. You'll never believe who it was."

As far as Clay was concerned, it didn't matter who it was. As long as they had a name they could find him.

"I give up. Just tell me."

"Trip Fitzgerald. It seems he's been dismissed from several jobs for inappropriate actions. Plus he was sued a couple of times, but the cases were all dismissed. Apparently, it became a he said/she said situation. In other words, he was hitting on the ladies, and when they didn't reciprocate he started following them."

"Got him!" Clay pumped a fist in the air. "What do we do next?"

"I'm calling the country club manager to see if they checked his references and to find out if they've had any complaints. We can't pick him up without probable cause. As far as I can tell he's kept his nose clean since he's been in town. Unless he's Maizie's stalker, of course."

"I was afraid you were going to say that. I have to get back to the boutique. I won't relax until I know she's safe."

"If you can wait a minute I'll go with you. Let me call Liza and get her to tap into the rumor mill. You know how efficient that thing is. If he's so much as swatted a butt she'll find out. I'd bet my bottom dollar he hasn't been a good boy. The recidivism rate on sexual offenders is incredibly high."

"I WANT YOU TO TAKE A ride with me," Trip said. Sure, it sounded like an invitation, but Maizie knew better.

"No!" she shrieked when he got a death grip on her wrist. "Let go of my arm!"

"I don't think so." It was said so casually you'd think they were discussing the weather. "You *are* going with me."

Although he wasn't a large man he was strong and very determined.

Terror was increasing her desperation, but neither

emotion was going to get her out of this mess. What Maizie wouldn't give for a machete, or a howitzer or even a butter knife. Unfortunately, she couldn't reach anything more lethal than a stapler.

"You really don't want to do this." She was trying to reason with him. Was she nuts? This lunatic wouldn't respond to anything other than sheer brute force. And where did that leave her? Up the creek, that's where.

"Yes, I do. I'm in love with you and we're going to spend a romantic weekend together. I know you don't love your husband. I've read all about it in the paper."

When he smiled, her gag reflex kicked in.

"You shouldn't believe everything you read." She returned his smile, trying to defuse the situation, but it didn't work.

"Don't screw with me." He brought his face in close to hers. "You're coming with me and I'm not terribly interested in your opinion." Trip emphasized his command by grabbing a handful of Maizie's hair. It was a show of domination that hurt like hell.

"Stop it!" She swatted at him, missing her mark by a mile.

"We don't have all day. Your stupid assistant will be back soon." He jerked Maizie's hair again, forcing her out from behind the counter.

Think, girl, think! She didn't have a weapon, so what did she have? Her brains—that was it. She'd have to outsmart him. She was *not* getting in a car with him.

She had to think self-defense. Talk to him. Get him to relax. Make him think she was his friend.

Deep breath. Get your brain in gear!

Other than a jewelry display, the only thing on the counter was a bottle of Ralph Lauren perfume. Maizie didn't know how she could use it, but she was running out of options.

Trip pulled a shiny, pointed stiletto from his pocket. Holy crap! Maizie had come to a knife fight armed with a bottle of Ralph. Those were bad odds.

"Move it!" He pushed Maizie toward the door.

If she went with him, she wouldn't be returning. Or if she did, it would be in a body bag. So for better or worse, she had to put up the fight of a lifetime.

When Maizie stumbled, he kicked her—and boy, that made her mad. The sadistic little bastard might win, but he was gonna find himself hurting.

Seconds later he managed to drag her to the back parking lot. The silver subcompact sitting next to her Mustang had to be his. It couldn't be any bigger than a smart car. What kind of idiot came to a kidnapping in Marian the Librarian's car? On TV the bad guys always used a nondescript white van—without windows. But this wasn't *CSI,* it was life or death.

"Trip. Think about it. You don't want to do this."

He responded with a grunt—so much for reasoning. He was as crazy as a loon.

Maizie's resolve strengthened, her spine stiffened and her calm returned with a vengeance. Trip Fitzgerald was going to wish he'd never met her. You didn't mess with a Westerfield twin and come out unscathed.

He hit the electric door locks and shoved her toward the vehicle. Maizie had already decided she wasn't going to get in his car, but when he popped the trunk her heart nearly jumped out of her chest.

He could wave his stiletto all he wanted—it didn't matter one bit. There was no way she'd fit in *that* trunk.

"Get in, right now!" He pushed her headfirst toward the gaping abyss. It couldn't be any bigger than two-by-two, and wouldn't hold a twenty-five-pound turkey. Even so it looked like a black hole, ready to suck her in.

Maizie was afraid she might faint but then her anger came back. If he wanted to stab her, so be it. She had righteous indignation and a ton of adrenaline on her side.

Maizie grabbed his ears and rammed her knee into his groin. To the casual observer it might have looked brutal, and yes, it probably was. Frankly, she hoped his gonads had taken up residence in his nasal cavity.

His scream was primal. His agony was apparent. And Maizie was happy as a clam. She slapped her hands together. It served him right.

CLAY AND ZACK PULLED INTO the parking lot in time to get an up close and personal look at Maizie's martial arts exhibition.

Zack winced as Trip collapsed on the pavement clutching his groin. "Ooh, that hurts."

Clay frankly didn't care two hoots about the bastard's pain. He was too focused on getting to Maizie and reassuring himself that she was okay.

"Do you suppose she needs some help?" Zack's question was clearly rhetorical. He hopped from the cruiser and jerked Trip off the ground. He slapped the cuffs on Mr. Fitzgerald with a certain amount of relish, read him his rights and tossed him in the back of the police car.

It was a darned good thing Zack was there, otherwise Clay would have been tempted to beat the crap out of the tennis pro. And Clay hadn't been in a fight since the ninth grade. That was the time Poochie Benton gave him a black eye and Clay had learned a valuable lesson—watch out for the wiry guys.

He enveloped his wife in a bear hug. "Oh, baby. I was so scared." He wasn't quite sure his heart would ever recover.

"Clay. Clay!" She hit him on the chest, trying to pull away.

"What?"

"I can't breathe."

"Oh." He reluctantly loosened his grip. He couldn't help feeling overwrought. It wasn't every day he had to watch his best girl take down a kidnapper.

"Sweetheart." He nuzzled her neck, inhaling the flowery scent of her hair. "I almost had a coronary when we drove up and I realized what was happening."

Maizie made a muffled sound he couldn't quite understand so he squeezed her a little tighter. It wasn't until she whacked him that he realized he was smothering her again.

"Sorry." Clay pushed back just far enough to make a thorough inspection. No blood. No visible bruises. That was a relief. Her hair was all messed up, but it merely looked as if she'd been running her hands through it.

"What exactly happened?"

It was a simple question. But if her sputtering was any indication, it wasn't one she could answer. Mary Stuart Walker had been silenced by shock and possibly some version of post-traumatic stress disorder. Clay didn't think it would last long.

By that time so many people were converging on the premises you'd think it was a tourist attraction. Zack had obviously called his wife, so naturally the entire family had heard about the fiasco. Mama was the first to arrive, quickly followed by Kenni and Liza.

"May I take Maizie home?" Clay asked Zack.

"Give me a second to disperse the mob. I need to ask her some questions and get a statement first." The sheriff turned to the crowd and made an announcement. "The excitement's over so everyone without a badge can head on out." When the gawkers left, Zack turned to his wife. "Liza, why don't you and your mother go inside and wait for me?"

"Okay," Liza replied steering Mama toward the door.

Maizie burrowed her head into Clay's chest. He could tell from the way she was shaking that she was close to hysteria.

Clay disentangled himself and led Maizie inside. "Where's PJ?" he asked.

"She went to the post office." Maizie wiped her nose on her sleeve. "She should be back in a few minutes."

Right on cue there was a ruckus at the front door. "Bubba Carter, you dolt, let me in!"

"The cavalry has arrived," Maizie said with the hint of a smile.

"Maizie, what happened?" PJ almost bowled her boss over with a huge hug. "There are cops and EMTs and your family. Can't I leave for five minutes without you getting into trouble?" She ended her tirade with a flood of tears.

"I'm okay," Maizie reassured her friend. "Trip Fitzgerald tried to kidnap me but I fought him off."

"The tennis pro tried to kidnap you!" PJ shouted.

"I'm afraid so."

"Ohmigod! What's happening to this town? A girl's not safe anywhere."

To forestall another diatribe, Maizie asked, "Would you mind closing up while I talk to Zack? Clay's going to take me home when that's done."

"Of course." PJ put her hands on her hips and spoke to Clay. "You pamper her, ya hear?"

"Yes, ma'am," Clay said with a mock salute.

MAIZIE WAS IN HEAVEN. What more could a girl want than a steamy bath and a cold glass of bubbly? The end of cellulite or world peace might be nice, but that was way outside her ability.

The water was cooling and she was starting to look like a California raisin so it was probably time to get back to the real world. She'd just wrapped herself in a towel when Clay strolled in and refilled her champagne flute.

"How are you feeling?" He ran his hands up her arms and caressed her shoulders.

"Better." Maizie wrapped her arms around his neck.

"That's good, really good," Clay muttered, keeping his eyes on her lips. He went for a soft exploratory kiss that quickly deepened until they were both having a hard time catching their breath. The old magic was back, and it was better than ever.

For what seemed like hours, although it was probably only minutes, Clay feasted on her body. She felt like a delectable treat, but that wasn't enough. Even in love, turnabout was fair play. Without regard for buttons, she ripped open his shirt, running her fingers through his chest hair.

"I love this." Maizie lowered her hands to massage his butt.

"And I love doing this." He leaned down to take her nipple into his mouth, sending shock waves through her.

That was the last of the conversation. Their lovemaking was a wonderful combination of youthful lust and mature passion. It was a reaffirmation of a marriage that had endured for more than two decades. Exhausted, Maizie and Clay were spooned prior to drifting off to sleep.

"I was terrified something horrible had happened to you," Clay murmured.

"I got a few gray hairs on that one, too," Maizie said with a giggle.

Clay kissed the side of her neck. "I don't know what I'd do if I lost you."

"It's a good thing you won't have to find out, isn't it? I'm not going anywhere. And for what it's worth I'm really sorry I started this whole thing by wanting to make you jealous. It was silly and immature."

"Don't worry. It's kind of funny now." So their marriage was back on its foundation—the ability to find humor in almost any situation.

Chapter Thirty-Five

It was almost two weeks before the brouhaha died down. Trip Fitzgerald remained in jail unable to meet an astronomical bail set by an irate judge and Maizie wasn't losing any sleep over it. As far she was concerned the dweeb could rot in the slammer. Society would be better off.

Clay's business problems had been resolved. The planner from hell had been sent off to harass some other poor sucker. The construction company was able to get on with the highway project and Clay's engineering firm was in the black. Yeah!

Hannah had come to grips with her mother's brush with crime. And last but certainly not least, the Walkers were back to being the most loving married couple in Magnolia Bluffs.

After hours of conversation, a few tears and, oh, yes, some memorable lovemaking, they came to an agreement about communication and not taking each other for granted. It was something they'd both needed to be reminded of.

Maizie admitted she was equally responsible for the

stagnation of their relationship and Clay vowed to be more open with his concerns, both personal and professional. It was a classic win-win situation.

But Maizie still had something up her sleeve.

It was Tuesday and that meant a cellulite-building and utterly delectable Southern breakfast at Daisy's Dining Spot with Kenni and Liza.

"I have an idea." Maizie took a sip of her coffee. "After everything we've gone through, I want to do something special for Clay. That's what I need your help with."

Kenni put her head in her hands. "Oh, boy."

Liza grimaced as she doctored her coffee, obviously seeking a sugar high.

After taking Trip Fitzgerald down—literally—Maizie had adopted a new attitude. It wasn't that she viewed herself as a super ninja, it was simply that she had renewed confidence. But this idea had nothing to do with woman power; it was about doing something special for the man she loved more than life itself. And who better to help her with it than her BFFs Liza and Kenni?

She explained her idea before asking for their opinion. "Am I crazy or do you think it will work?"

"Let me get this straight." Liza rubbed the bridge of her nose. "You want to lure Clay out to the baseball field to renew your vows on the pitcher's mound, and you want to make it a surprise. Do I have that right?"

Kenni didn't say a word—she didn't have to, her opinion was written all over her face. She thought her cousin had truly lost her mind. Actually that wasn't out of the realm of possibility.

"I understand why you'd want to renew your vows," Liza said, "but I don't quite get the baseball field part. What's that about?"

Maizie called the waitress over to order a tea refill. "You remember when I tossed Clay's stuff out on the curb."

Kenni piped up. "That would be hard to forget."

Maizie ignored her cousin's sarcasm. "When I did that, I accidentally threw away his Little League national championship trophy." She had the grace to look sheepish. "And it sort of got squashed."

"Pray tell, how did a metal trophy 'sort of get squashed'?" Liza asked.

"I'm not real sure," Maizie admitted. "A guy in a Camaro came along and started rummaging through Clay's belongings. I ran him off but after he sped away the trophy was in the middle of the road in pieces. Then Clay arrived and had a fit about how I'd ruined his Little League memories. He tossed the rest of his stuff in the truck and hauled butt, leaving me with the bits and pieces of the trophy."

"So where's this monument to pre-adolescent baseball accomplishment now?" Kenni asked.

"And do you have all the parts?" Liza asked.

"I think so," Maizie answered. Then the light dawned. She knew where her friends were going with their questions. "Do you think I can get it fixed?"

"Let's go to Atlanta and see if we can find a miracle worker," Liza said. "Then we can discuss the shindig at the ball field. A surprise vow renewal. What an amazing idea. I wouldn't miss it for the world."

It took several days before they could coordinate their schedules to include a trip to Dave's Trophy Shop in Atlanta. Once they got there, the prognosis was dire.

"I don't know." Dave's accent was pure South Georgia. "This bad boy is plum messed up. Whatcha do, run over it with a lawn mower?" He cackled over his own not-so-funny joke.

"Actually, it was a Camaro," Maizie said wryly.

"A Camaro?" He evidently thought that was even more hilarious and cackled even louder.

"Let's get down to business." Liza took charge. "Can you fix it? And how long will it take?" She didn't bother to ask about the price.

The shopkeeper scratched his head. "Give me a couple of days." He quoted a fee that made Maizie's eyes pop. Did she look like she was made of money? Hadn't she learned her lesson with Trina's overpriced stink bomb?

After they finished haggling over price and completion date, Maizie was exhausted. She would never make it at the Chicago Board of Trade.

"Let's go have a piña colada," she suggested to her partners in crime. "After everything that's happened, I think I deserve a little pampering. My treat."

Chapter Thirty-Six

It was the weekend before Thanksgiving and the forecast for Saturday was clear and crisp—thank goodness. Maizie had been agonizing over the weather for days. Conditions that time of the year could be iffy and considering how many people she'd invited, including their extended families, all their colleagues and the entire Walker and Tucker Little League team she'd be in a big mess if it rained.

The preparations for this production had been mindboggling. Liza was in charge of invitations, Mama was handling the caterers, Kenni was coordinating with the parks department and the Little League and Hannah was responsible for keeping her mouth shut. Maizie's job was to coordinate the decorations and make sure Clay showed up. It had been a major undertaking and they had one more day to complete the preparations.

"Mama, is everything a go?" Maizie was multitasking by talking on the phone and blowing up hundreds of balloons with a portable helium machine. The back room of the Boudoir was awash in bobbing color.

"The catering tent is up and the cooks are ready to go. I have my assigned duties under control. How about you?"

That was a good question. Maizie was questioning her sanity. What was wrong with reserving the church and having a classy ceremony followed by a family-only reception at the country club? That's what a normal person would do. However, it had been a long time since anyone had accused her of being ordinary.

"I'm fine." Maizie glanced at the dozens of balloons floating around above her head. "I think," she muttered.

"How do you plan to get him to the baseball field?"

She had that one nailed at least. "Harvey's going to help. He told Clay that their Little League team is having a fund-raiser washing cars and they want the sponsors to be there."

"Isn't it awfully cold to be washing cars?" Mama asked. She was always the first to pick up on the details.

"Whatever. I can't come up with anything else, so that's what we're going with. We'll show up around three, so I'm counting on you guys to get everything together."

"Don't worry about a thing, baby girl. All you have to do is make sure you get Clay there. You can't do the vows without him. Oh, and have fun."

Eleanor was a party-throwing diva, so Maizie wasn't concerned about that aspect. She was more worried about how Clay would react.

When she'd first come up with the picnic scheme, it had seemed brilliant. Now Maizie wasn't quite so sure. Would Clay like it or would he think it was another one of her hare-brained ideas?

It was too late to back out now. They'd ordered enough hot dogs to feed a small country and Hannah was on her way home.

BY THE TIME SATURDAY ROLLED around Maizie's nerves were stretched to the breaking point. She'd cleaned the kitchen, mopped the floors, vacuumed and paced. She was as nervous as a cat in a room full of rocking chairs.

Clay put his arms around her waist. "Is something wrong?"

"Why would you say that?" she snapped.

He answered with a raised eyebrow.

"No, there's nothing wrong." She was a terrible liar.

"I'm going to run down to the hardware store to get some paint. Since we don't have anything planned for the day, I thought I'd redo the fence."

Maizie was tempted to scream, but instead went for nonchalance. "That's great." She smacked her head. "Oh, wait. Harvey wants you to meet him at the ball park for the car wash, remember?"

"Oh, yeah. I guess I can't bag on that, huh?"

"No. I don't think so. What time are you heading out?"

Clay glanced at the clock. "Around two-thirty. The car wash isn't till three."

"Mind if I tag along? The boys are so cute. After that we can get something to eat." Talk about lame. He must see right through her.

Clay gave her a strange look, but nodded. "Okay. It doesn't sound like your kind of thing, but if you want to come, that's fine. I think I'll take a shower first."

Maizie waited until Clay was upstairs before she

grabbed the phone to call her sister. "Liza, I'm driving myself nuts. Is everything okay down there?"

"Don't worry, we have it under control."

"He wanted to paint the fence!" Maizie wailed.

There was silence on the other end of the line before Liza spoke. "You nipped that in the bud, didn't you?"

"Of course," she barked. "I'm sorry. I'm being crazy. I'll see you in a little while." Maizie ran upstairs to change clothes. If she was lucky Clay wouldn't realize she'd put on a new outfit. He was a guy, why would he start noticing stuff like that now?

"WHAT DO YOU THINK is goin' on?" Clay asked as they pulled into the parking lot next to the Little League field.

"I don't know. This is your gig." Maizie tried to keep her voice even.

"It looks like they're having a festival." He put the car in Park, but didn't turn off the engine. "I'm not in the mood to wade through a crowd of people to watch a pumpkin pie eating contest." He groaned and Maizie could tell he would've been happier to paint the darned fence.

Too bad. "I don't know about you, but I'm going to see what's happening."

Clay looked surprised but didn't argue with her.

WHAT IN THE HECK was going on? Everywhere he looked there were people he knew, and they were all smiling. Something strange was afoot, and Clay had the sinking feeling he was the only person in town who wasn't in the loop.

"Do we have tickets to this thing?"

"Don't need 'em. Come with me." Maizie pulled him toward the largest of the three tents. "What do you think this is?" She pointed to the interior of the pavilion, which was decorated like a wedding chapel. The other tents had been prepared for the reception/picnic.

"I get it." He snapped his fingers. "It's a tent revival." There was a pulpit up front so that was the most logical answer he could dredge up on short notice.

"Nope. Try again."

"A circus? I saw a clown out front, didn't I?"

"Not quite," Maizie said and then muttered, "at least not yet."

Clay threw up his hands in surrender. "I give."

About that time Liza and Kenni strolled up, their husbands in tow. "Have you told him yet?" Liza asked excitedly.

Zack laid a hand on Clay's shoulder. "Keep in mind the guys had nothing to do with this."

His comment was enough to make Clay want to run. What was *this?*

"Honey, remember when we sort of discussed renewing our vows?" Maizie asked.

"Uh-huh."

"Well." She put on what looked like a well-rehearsed smile. "We're going to."

"Going to what?"

"We're going to get remarried. Right here. In front of everyone." She did a wave that encompassed the entire ball field including the tents, their families, the clown and the Little League team.

Once Clay started laughing he couldn't stop. Finally

he was able to take a deep breath and get control of his mirth.

"You planned all of this and managed to keep it a secret from me? In Magnolia Bluffs? Unbelievable." He pulled Maizie to his side and kissed the top of her head. "So that's what the new outfit is all about."

"You noticed?" Maizie seemed confused by his observation.

"Of course. I'm always aware of what you're wearing.

Now her jaw literally dropped.

"So what do you say?" she asked. Her natural confidence had turned into sheepish uncertainty.

"I say yes." As if there was any question. He twirled her around to the applause of all the folks who had come to help them celebrate. Then he noticed Hannah standing by the edge of the crowd.

"Hey, sweetie! Were you in on this, too?"

Hannah gave him a hug. "We kept it a secret, didn't we?"

"That you did." He put his arms around his two best girls. "You ladies are sneaky." Life couldn't get any better.

"What's with the ball players?" he asked.

"Oh, that's right. Come here, guys."

Although the entire team came forward, the guy leading the pack was the pitcher. "Hey, Mr. Walker. Your wife wants us to give you this." He handed Clay a large gift-wrapped package.

Clay was at a loss. What was Maizie up to now? When he pulled out his old baseball trophy—albeit not quite in its original condition—Clay grabbed his wife, leaned her back over his arm and gave her a kiss their friends and loved ones would be talking about for years. That was the day Maizie and Clay Walker re-newed their vows and treated the citizens of Magnolia Bluffs to a party they wouldn't soon forget.

* * * * *

Harlequin is 60 years old, and Harlequin Blaze is celebrating!
After all, a lot can happen in 60 years, or 60 minutes...or 60 seconds!
Find out what's going down in Blaze's heart-stopping new mini-series,
FROM 0 TO 60!
Getting from "Hello" to "How was it?" can happen fast....

Here's a sneak peek of the first book,
A LONG, HARD RIDE
by Alison Kent
Available March 2009.

"Is THAT FOR ME?" Trey asked.

Cardin Worth cocked her head to the side and considered how much better the day already seemed. "Good morning to you, too."

When she didn't hold out the second cup of coffee for him to take, he came closer. She sipped from her heavy white mug, hiding her grin and her giddy rush of nerves behind it.

But when he stopped in front of her, she made the mistake of lowering her gaze from his face to the exposed strip of his chest. It was either give him his cup of coffee or bury her nose against him and breathe in. She remembered so clearly how he smelled. How he tasted.

She gave him his coffee.

After taking a quick gulp, he smiled and said, "Good morning, Cardin. I hope the floor wasn't too hard for you."

The hardness of the floor hadn't been the problem. She shook her head. "Are you kidding? I slept like a baby, swaddled in my sleeping bag."

"In my sleeping bag, you mean."

If he wanted to get technical, yeah. "Thanks for the loaner. It made sleeping on the floor almost bearable." As had the warmth of his spooned body, she thought, then quickly changed the subject. "I saw you have a loaf of bread and some eggs. Would you like me to cook breakfast?"

He lowered his coffee mug slowly, his gaze as warm as the sun on her shoulders, as the ceramic heating her hands. "I didn't bring you out here to wait on me."

"You didn't bring me out here at all. I volunteered to come."

"To help me get ready for the race. Not to serve me."

"It's just breakfast, Trey. And coffee." Even if last night it had been more. Even if the way he was looking at her made her want to climb back into that sleeping bag. "I work much better when my stomach's not growling. I thought it might be the same for you."

"It is, but I'll cook. You made the coffee."

"That's because I can't work at all without caffeine."

"If I'd known that, I would've put on a pot as soon I got up."

"What time *did* you get up?" Judging by the sun's position, she swore it couldn't be any later than seven now. And, yeah, they'd agreed to start working at six.

"Maybe four?" he guessed, giving her a lazy smile.

"But it was almost two…" She let the sentence dangle, finishing the thought privately. She was quite sure he knew exactly what time they'd finally fallen asleep after he'd made love to her.

The question facing her now was where did this relationship—if you could even call it *that*—go from here?

* * * * *

Cardin and Trey are about to find out that great sex is only the beginning....
Don't miss the fireworks!
Get ready for
A LONG, HARD RIDE
by Alison Kent.
Available March 2009,
wherever Blaze books are sold.

You're invited to join our Tell Harlequin Reader Panel!

By joining our new reader panel you will:

- Receive Harlequin® books—they are FREE and yours to keep with no obligation to purchase anything!
- Participate in fun online surveys
- Exchange opinions and ideas with women just like you
- Have a say in our new book ideas and help us publish the best in women's fiction

In addition, you will have a chance to win great prizes and receive special gifts!
See Web site for details. Some conditions apply.
Space is limited.

To join, visit us at

www.TellHarlequin.com.

REQUEST YOUR FREE BOOKS!

2 FREE NOVELS PLUS 2
FREE GIFTS!

Love, Home & Happiness!

HARLEQUIN Romance®

This February the Harlequin® Romance series
will feature six Diamond Brides stories featuring
diamond proposals and gorgeous grooms.

Share your dream wedding proposal and you could WIN!

The most romantic entry will win a diamond
necklace and will inspire a proposal in one of
our upcoming Diamond Grooms books in 2010.

In 100 words or less, tell us the most romantic
way that you dream of being proposed to.

For more information, and to enter
the Diamond Brides Proposal contest, please visit
www.DiamondBridesProposal.com

Or mail your entry to us at:

IN THE U.S.: 3010 Walden Ave., P.O. Box 9069, Buffalo, NY 14269-9069
IN CANADA: 225 Duncan Mill Road, Don Mills, ON M3B 3K9

www.eHarlequin.com   HRCONTESTFEB09

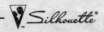

SPECIAL EDITION

TRAVIS'S APPEAL

by *USA TODAY* bestselling author

MARIE FERRARELLA

Shana O'Reilly couldn't deny it—family lawyer
Travis Marlowe had some kind of appeal. But
as Travis handled her father's tricky estate
planning, he discovered things weren't what
they seemed in the O'Reilly clan. Would
an explosive secret leave Travis and Shana's
budding relationship in tatters?

*Available March 2009
wherever books are sold.*

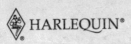

HARLEQUIN®

American ★ Romance®

COMING NEXT MONTH
Available March 10, 2009

#1249 THE SHERIFF OF HORSESHOE, TEXAS by Linda Warren
Men Made in America
Quiet, friendly Horseshoe is the perfect place for Wyatt Carson to raise his young daughter. Until Peyton Ross zooms through his Texas hometown, disrupting his peaceful Sunday and turning his world upside down. The irrepressible blonde is tempting the widowed lawman to let loose and start living again. But there's more to this fun-loving party girl than meets the eye....

#1250 THE TRIPLETS' RODEO MAN by Tina Leonard
The Morgan Men
Cricket Jasper knows Jack Morgan's all wrong for her. But that doesn't stop the virtuous deacon from falling for the sexy rodeo rider. The firstborn Morgan son came home to make things right with his estranged father. Now *he's* about to become a father. Whoever dreamed it would take a loving woman with three babies on the way to catch this roving cowboy?

#1251 TWINS FOR THE TEACHER by Michele Dunaway
Times Two
Ever since Hank Friesen enrolled his son and daughter in Nolter Elementary, Jolie Tomlinson has been finding it hard to resist the ten-year-old twins...*and* their sexy dad. The fourth-grade teacher is happy to help out the workaholic widower—but getting involved with the father of her students is definitely against the rules. Besides, Jolie doesn't know if she's ready to be a mother—not until she tells Hank about her past....

#1252 OOH, BABY! by Ann Roth
Running a business and being a temporary mother to her sister's seven-month-old are *two* full-time jobs. The last thing Lily Gleason needs is to be audited! Then she meets her new accountant. Carter Boyle is handsome, single and trustworthy...and already smitten with Lily's infant niece. But the CPA has a precious secret—one that could make or break Lily's trust in him.

www.eHarlequin.com

HARCNMBPA0209